Chris,

I love you dearly,

Deb

Happy Birthday, 2018

THE WINGED ENERGY
OF DELIGHT

BOOKS BY ROBERT BLY

Poetry

Silence in the Snowy Fields
The Light Around the Body
The Man in the Black Coat Turns
Loving a Woman in Two Worlds
Meditations on the Insatiable Soul
Morning Poems
Eating the Honey of Words: New and Selected Poems
The Night Abraham Called to the Stars

Anthologies

The Rag and Bone Shop of the Heart (with James Hillman
and Michael Meade)
News of the Universe: Poems of Twofold Consciousness
The Soul Is Here for Its Own Joy

Prose

Talking All Morning (Interviews)
The Eight Stages of Translation
A Little Book on the Human Shadow (with William Booth)
Iron John: A Book About Men
The Sibling Society
The Maiden King: The Reunion of Masculine and Feminine
(with Marion Woodman)

Translations

The Kabir Book: 44 of the Ecstatic Poems of Kabir
Selected Poems of Rainer Maria Rilke
Times Alone: Selected Poems of Antonio Machado
Neruda and Vallejo: Selected Poems (with James Wright and John Knoepfle)
Lorca and Jiménez: Selected Poems
When Grapes Turn to Wine (Rumi)
The Lightning Should Have Fallen on Ghalib (with Sunil Dutta)

THE WINGED ENERGY
OF DELIGHT

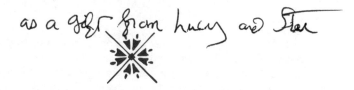

Selected Translations

Robert Bly

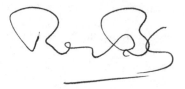

HarperCollins*Publishers*

HarperCollins books may be purchased for educational, business, or sales promotional use. For information, please write: Special Markets Department, HarperCollins Publishers Inc., 10 East 53rd Street, New York, NY 10022.

FIRST EDITION

Designed by Nicola Ferguson

Printed on acid-free paper

Library of Congress Cataloging-in-Publication Data

The winged energy of delight: selected translations / [translated by] Robert Bly.—1st ed.
    p.   cm.
  ISBN 0-06-057582-4 (alk. paper)
    1. Poetry—Translations into English.   2. Poetry—Collections.
    I. Bly, Robert.

PN6101.W44   2004
808.81—dc22   2003067619

04 05 06 07 08 NMSG/RRD 10 9 8 7 6 5 4 3 2 1

CONTENTS

SOME WORDS ABOUT THIS BOOK

DURING THE FIFTIES, there was very little sense in the poetry community of contemporary European and South American poetry. While in Norway a few years later I found Paal Brekke's anthology *Modernistisk Lyrikk* (*The Modern Poem*). He included one poem apiece by seven or eight lively poets from each of the major European countries. There was a great freshness in many of these poets. How was it that I had never seen the names of Trakl, Ekelöf, or Vallejo in contemporary American magazines? Many of these poets engaged in an explosive attention to metaphor.

Back in the United States, after driving away one day to a distant library to find a copy of a Tranströmer book called *Den Halvfärdiga Himlen* (*Half-Finished Heaven*), I found on my return a letter from Tranströmer directed to James Wright, a poem of whose he had read in *The Times Literary Supplement*. So some poets in Europe were alert to any movement in the world of the image. I soon translated some of Tomas Tranströmer's poems, and James Wright and I did the first book of Trakl's poems into English. Later we translated Vallejo, Neruda, and Jiménez together. Translating allows one to go deeply into the adventures taking place inside another person's poem; translating with friends is one of the greatest pleasures in the world.

Wright and I depended on Hardie St. Martin, who had a Spanish-speaking mother and an American father, and knew both languages in the cradle. His care and love lie behind all our translations from the Spanish. Tranströmer, whose English is excellent, gave me much help on English versions of his poems. I had no help on Rilke, and depended on my own German, which was probably not good enough. In a little book called *The Eight Stages of Translation,* I follow a single sonnet of Rilke's through the eight stages that I detected from my own practice. This booklet attempts to show how complicated the process of translation is, and how many errors one can fall into. When I have had no help with the language at all, as was the case with my early work on Kabir, I call those poems "versions" instead of translations. My Kabir poems are rewritings of the translations into colonial English made by Rabindranath Tagore in the 1920s. Even in his stodgy English, one could feel the astounding courage and brilliance of Kabir. The Mirabai poems have evolved from word-by-word translations which were given to me by the East Asian Language Department of the University of Chicago. For the Ghalib poems, my son-in-law, Sunil Dutta, made literal translations from the Hindi with elaborate commentaries in English on each line. In my still more recent translations of Hafez, I have had help from an unfailingly fierce and generous scholar of Iranian literature, Leonard Lewisohn.

When Hugh Van Dusen at HarperCollins first suggested that I gather together a large group of my translations in a single book, I was delighted to have the chance. But given that twenty-two poets were to be included, it wasn't at all clear in what order they should come. Arrangement by birthdate didn't seem right, because the book would then begin with Horace, but Horace is most interesting to people familiar with the work done during recent decades on the image and its importance in argument. Arranging the poems by the order in which my translations got published didn't make sense either, because some translations had to wait years. Finally, my daughter, Bridget, said, "Why don't you publish them in the order in which you first loved them?" That idea is the one I settled on for this book.

The most important gift we receive when translating is to see genius—in Mirabai, Rumi, Lorca, Ponge—shine straight through into the world.

THE WINGED ENERGY
OF DELIGHT

TOMAS TRANSTRÖMER

TOMAS TRANSTRÖMER COMES from a long line of ship pilots who worked in and around the Stockholm Archipelago. He is at home on islands. His face is thin and angular, and the swift, spare face reminds one of Hans Christian Andersen's or the younger Kierkegaard's. He has a strange genius for the image—images come up almost effortlessly. The images flow upward like water rising in some lonely place, in the swamps, or deep fir woods.

Swedish poetry tends to be very rational, and therefore open to fads. Tranströmer, simply by publishing his books, leads a movement of poetry in the opposite direction, toward a poetry of silence and depths.

One of the most beautiful qualities in his poems is the space we feel in them. I think one reason for that is that the four or five main images that appear in each of his poems come from widely separated sources in the psyche. His poems are a sort of railway station where trains that have come enormous distances stand briefly in the same building. One train may have some Russian snow still lying on the undercarriage, and another may have Mediterranean flowers still fresh in the compartments, and Ruhr soot on the roofs.

The poems are mysterious because of the distance the images have come to get there. Mallarmé believed there should be mystery in poetry, and urged poets to get it by removing the links that tie the poem to its occasion in the real world. Tranströmer keeps the link to the worldly occasion, and yet the poems have a mystery and surprise that never fade, even on many readings.

Rilke taught that poets should be "bees of the invisible." Making honey for the invisible suggests that the poet remain close to earthly history, but move as well toward the spiritual and the invisible. Tranströmer suspects that as an artist he is merely a way for "the Memory" to get out into the world. Even at seventeen he was aware that the dead "wanted to have their portrait painted." Somehow that cannot be done without making peace with rhetoric. He wants to tell of spiritual matters, but he doesn't want to be a preacher. If rhetoric could kill Christianity in Sweden, maybe it could kill poetry as well. In "From an African Diary," he describes climbing on a canoe hollowed from a log:

> The canoe is incredibly wobbly, even when you sit on your heels.
> A balancing act. If you have the heart on the left side you have
> to lean a bit to the right, nothing in the pockets, no big arm
> movements, please, all rhetoric has to be left behind. Precisely:
> rhetoric is impossible here. The canoe glides out over the water.

In "The Scattered Congregation," Tranströmer remarks:

> Nicodemus the sleepwalker is on his way
> to the Address. Who's got the Address?
> Don't know. But that's where we're going.

TOMAS TRANSTRÖMER was born in Stockholm on April 15, 1931. His father and mother divorced when he was three; he and his mother lived after that in an apartment in the working-class district of Stockholm. He describes the apartment in the poem called "The Bookcase."

The early fifties were a rather formal time, both here and in Sweden, and Tranströmer began by writing concentrated, highly formal poems, some in iambs and some in the Alcaic meter. His first book, *17 Poems,* published in 1954, glowed with strange baroque elements, and contained only a few poems, but people noticed the power of the book immediately.

For several years, he worked as a psychologist in a boys' prison in Linköping, and then in 1965, he moved with his wife, Monica, and his two daughters, Paula and Emma, to Västerås, a town about forty miles west of Stockholm. He continued to work as a psychologist, this time for a labor organization funded by the State. He helped juvenile delinquents to reenter society and persons with physical disabilities to choose a career, and he counseled parole offenders and those in drug rehabilitation.

Tomas Tranströmer's poems are so luminous that genuine poetry can travel to another language and thrive. His poems have been translated into dozens of European and Asian languages; at this moment, something like thirty-eight.

The praise for his poems has steadily grown both in Europe and in the United States. He has received most of the important poetry prizes in Europe, including the Petrarch Prize in Germany, the Bonnier Award for Poetry, the Pilot Prize in 1988, the Nordic Council Prize in 1990, the Swedish Academy's Nordic Prize in 1991, and the Horst Bieneck Prize in 1992.

The town of Västerås recently had a formal farewell celebration in the old castle for Tomas and Monica, who were moving to Stockholm. A choir sang to him, and presents were piled up five feet high around his chair.

Today, the couple live in an apartment in Stockholm overlooking the harbor, near the old neighborhood where Tomas lived as a boy.

TRACK

2 A.M.: moonlight. The train has stopped
out in a field. Far-off sparks of light from a town,
flickering coldly on the horizon.

As when a man goes so deep into his dream
he will never remember that he was there
when he returns again to his room.

Or when a person goes so deep into a sickness
that his days all become some flickering sparks, a swarm,
feeble and cold on the horizon.

The train is entirely motionless.
2 o'clock: strong moonlight, few stars.

ALLEGRO

After a black day, I play Haydn,
and feel a little warmth in my hands.

The keys are ready. Kind hammers fall.
The sound is spirited, green, and full of silence.

The sound says that freedom exists
and someone pays no taxes to Caesar.

I shove my hands in my haydnpockets
and act like a man who is calm about it all.

I raise my haydnflag. The signal is:
"We do not surrender. But want peace."

The music is a house of glass standing on a slope;
rocks are flying, rocks are rolling.

The rocks roll straight through the house
but every pane of glass is still whole.

MORNING BIRD SONGS

I wake up my car;
pollen covers the windshield.
I put my dark glasses on.
The bird songs all turn dark.

Meanwhile someone is buying a paper
at the railroad station
not far from a big freight car
reddened all over with rust.
It shimmers in the sun.

The whole universe is full.

A cool corridor cuts through the spring warmth;
a man comes hurrying past
describing how someone right up in the main office
has been telling lies about him.

Through a backdoor in the landscape
the magpie arrives,
black and white, bird of the death-goddess.
A blackbird flies back and forth
until the whole scene becomes a charcoal drawing,
except for the white clothes on the line:
a Palestrina choir.

The whole universe is full!

Fantastic to feel how my poem is growing
while I myself am shrinking.
It's getting bigger, it's taking my place,
it's pressing against me.
It has shoved me out of the nest.
The poem is finished.

OUT IN THE OPEN

1

Late autumn labyrinth.
At the entry to the woods a thrown-away bottle.
Go in. Woods are silent abandoned houses this time of year.
Just a few sounds now: as if someone were moving twigs around
    carefully with pincers
or as if an iron hinge were whining feebly inside a thick trunk.
Frost has breathed on the mushrooms and they have shriveled up.
They look like objects and clothing left behind by people who've
    disappeared.
It will be dark soon. The thing to do now is to get out
and find the landmarks again: the rusty machine out in the field
and the house on the other side of the lake, a reddish square intense as
    a bouillon cube.

2

A letter from America drove me out again, started me walking
through the luminous June night in the empty suburban streets
among newborn districts without memories, cool as blueprints.

Letter in my pocket. Half-mad, lost walking, it is a kind of prayer.
Over there evil and good actually have faces.
For the most part with us it's a fight between roots, numbers, shades
    of light.

The people who run death's errands for him don't shy from daylight.
They rule from glass offices. They mill about in the bright sun.
They lean forward over a desk, and throw a look to the side.

Far off I found myself standing in front of one of the new buildings.
Many windows flowed together there into a single window.
In it the luminous nightsky was caught, and the walking trees.
It was a mirrorlike lake with no waves, turned on edge in the
    summer night.

Violence seemed unreal
for a few moments.

3
Sun burning. The plane comes in low
throwing a shadow shaped like a giant cross that rushes over the
    ground.
A man is sitting in the field poking at something.
The shadow arrives.
For a fraction of a second he is right in the center of the cross.

I have seen the cross hanging in the cool church vaults.
At times it resembles a split-second snapshot of something
moving at tremendous speed.

SOLITUDE

1

Right here I was nearly killed one night in February.
My car slewed on the ice, sideways,
into the other lane. The oncoming cars —
their headlights — came nearer.

My name, my daughters, my job
slipped free and fell behind silently,
farther and farther back. I was anonymous,
like a schoolboy in a lot surrounded by enemies.

The approaching traffic had powerful lights.
They shone on me while I turned and turned
the wheel in a transparent fear that moved like eggwhite.
The seconds lengthened out — making more room —
they grew long as hospital buildings.

It felt as if you could just take it easy
and loaf a bit
before the smash came.

Then firm land appeared: a helping sandgrain
or a marvelous gust of wind. The car took hold
and fishtailed back across the road.
A signpost shot up, snapped off — a ringing sound —
tossed into the dark.

Came all quiet. I sat there in my seat belt
and watched someone tramp through the blowing snow
to see what had become of me.

2

I have been walking awhile
on the frozen Swedish fields
and I have seen no one.

In other parts of the world
people are born, live, and die
in a constant human crush.

To be visible all the time—to live
in a swarm of eyes—
surely that leaves its mark on the face.
Features overlaid with clay.

The low voices rise and fall
as they divide up
heaven, shadows, grains of sand.

I have to be by myself
ten minutes every morning,
ten minutes every night,
—and nothing to be done!

We all line up to ask each other for help.

Millions.
One.

THE SCATTERED CONGREGATION

1

We got ready and showed our home.
The visitor thought: you live well.
The slum must be inside you.

2

Inside the church, pillars and vaulting
white as plaster, like the cast
around the broken arm of faith.

3

Inside the church there's a begging bowl
that slowly lifts from the floor
and floats along the pews.

4

But the church bells have gone underground.
They're hanging in the sewage pipes.
Whenever we take a step, they ring.

5

Nicodemus the sleepwalker is on his way
to the Address. Who's got the Address?
Don't know. But that's where we're going.

AT FUNCHAL

(Island of Madeira)

On the beach there's a seafood place, simple, a shack thrown up by survivors of the shipwreck. Many turn back at the door, but not the sea winds. A shadow stands deep inside his smoky hut frying two fish according to an old recipe from Atlantis, tiny garlic explosions, oil running over sliced tomatoes, every morsel says that the ocean wishes us well, a humming from the deep places.

She and I look into each other. It's like climbing the wild-flowered mountain slopes without feeling the least bit tired. We've sided with the animals, they welcome us, we don't age. But we have experienced so much together over the years, including those times when we weren't so good (as when we stood in line to give blood to the healthy giant—he said he wanted a transfusion), incidents which should have separated us if they hadn't united us, and incidents which we've totally forgotten— though they haven't forgotten us! They've turned to stones, dark and light, stones in a scattered mosaic. And now it happens: the pieces move toward each other, the mosaic appears and is whole. It waits for us. It glows down from the hotel-room wall, some figure violent and tender. Perhaps a face, we can't take it all in as we pull off our clothes.

After dusk we go out. The dark powerful paw of the cape lies thrown out into the sea. We walk in swirls of human beings, we are cuffed around kindly, among soft tyrannies, everyone chatters excitedly in the foreign tongue. "No man is an island." We gain strength from *them,* but also from ourselves. From what is inside that the other person can't see. That which can only meet itself. The innermost paradox, the underground garage flowers, the vent toward the good dark. A drink that bubbles in an empty glass. An amplifier that magnifies silence. A path that grows over after every step. A book that can only be read in the dark.

SCHUBERTIANA

1

Outside New York, a high place where with one glance you take in the houses where eight million human beings live.

The giant city over there is a long flimmery drift, a spiral galaxy seen from the side.

Inside the galaxy, coffee cups are being pushed across the desk, department store windows beg, a whirl of shoes that leave no trace behind.

Fire escapes climbing up, elevator doors that silently close, behind triple-locked doors a steady swell of voices.

Slumped-over bodies doze in subway cars, catacombs in motion.

I know also—statistics to the side—that at this instant in some room down there Schubert is being played, and for that person the notes are more real than all the rest.

2

The immense treeless plains of the human brain have gotten folded and refolded 'til they are the size of a fist.

The swallow in April returns to its last year's nest under the eaves in precisely the right barn in precisely the right township.

She flies from the Transvaal, passes the equator, flies for six weeks over two continents, navigates toward precisely this one disappearing dot in the landmass.

And the man who gathers up the signals from a whole lifetime into a few rather ordinary chords for five string musicians

the one who got a river to flow through the eye of a needle

is a plump young man from Vienna, his friends called him "The Mushroom," who slept with his glasses on

and every morning punctually stood at his high writing table.

When he did that the wonderful centipedes started to move on the page.

3

The five instruments play. I go home through warm woods where the
earth is springy under my feet,

curl up like someone still unborn, sleep, roll on so weightlessly into
the future, suddenly understand that plants are thinking.

How much we have to take on trust every minute we live in order not
to drop through the earth!

Take on trust the snow masses clinging to rocksides over the town.

Take on trust the unspoken promises, and the smile of agreement,
trust that the telegram does not concern us, and that the sudden ax
blow from inside is not coming.

Trust the axles we ride on down the thruway among the swarm of
steel bees magnified three hundred times.

But none of that stuff is really worth the trust we have.

The five string instruments say that we can take something else on
trust, and they walk with us a bit on the road.

As when the lightbulb goes out on the stair, and the hand follows—
trusting it—the blind banister rail that finds its way in the dark.

4

We crowd up onto the piano stool and play four-handed in f-minor,
two drivers for the same carriage, it looks a little ridiculous.

It looks as if the hands are moving weights made of sound back and
forth, as if we were moving lead weights

in an attempt to alter the big scale's frightening balance: happiness
and suffering weigh exactly the same.

Annie said, "This music is so heroic," and she is right.

But those who glance enviously at men of action, people who despise
themselves inside for not being murderers,

do not find themselves in this music.

And the people who buy and sell others, and who believe that
everyone can be bought, don't find themselves here.

Not their music. The long melody line that remains itself among all its
   variations, sometimes shiny and gentle, sometimes rough and
   powerful, the snail's trace and steel wire.
The stubborn humming sound that this instant is with us
upward into
the depths.

VERMEER

It's not a sheltered world. The noise begins over there, on the other
    side of the wall
where the alehouse is
with its laughter and quarrels, its rows of teeth, its tears, its chiming of
    clocks,
and the psychotic brother-in-law, the murderer, in whose presence
    everyone feels fear.

The huge explosion and the emergency crew arriving late,
boats showing off on the canals, money slipping down into pockets—
    the wrong man's—
ultimatum piled on ultimatum,
widemouthed red flowers whose sweat reminds us of approaching
    war.

And then straight through the wall—from there—straight into the
    airy studio
and the seconds that have got permission to live for centuries.
Paintings that choose the name: "The Music Lesson"
or "A Woman in Blue Reading a Letter."
She is eight months pregnant, two hearts beating inside her.
The wall behind her holds a crinkly map of Terra Incognita.

Just breathe. An unidentifiable blue fabric has been tacked to the
    chairs.
Gold-headed tacks flew in with astronomical speed
and stopped smack there
as if they had always been stillness and nothing else.

The ears experience a buzz, perhaps it's depth or perhaps height.
It's the pressure from the other side of the wall,
the pressure that makes each fact float
and makes the brushstroke firm.

Passing through walls hurts human beings, they get sick from it,
but we have no choice.
It's all one world. Now to the walls.
The walls are a part of you.
One either knows that, or one doesn't; but it's the same for everyone
except for small children. There aren't any walls for them.

The airy sky has taken its place leaning against the wall.
It is like a prayer to what is empty.
And what is empty turns its face to us
and whispers:
"I am not empty, I am open."

APRIL AND SILENCE

Spring lies abandoned.
A ditch the color of dark violet
moves alongside me
giving no images back.

The only thing that shines
are some yellow flowers.

I am carried inside
my own shadow like a violin
in its black case.

The only thing I want to say
hovers just out of reach
like the family silver
at the pawnbroker's.

DECEMBER EVENING, '72

Here I come the invisible man, perhaps in the employ
of some huge Memory that wants to live at this moment. And I drive by

the white church that's locked up. A saint made of wood is inside,
smiling helplessly, as if someone had taken his glasses.

He's alone. Everything else is now, now, now. Gravity
pulling us toward work in the dark and the bed at night. The war.

MIRABAI

WHEN MIRABAI COMES to meet you, you'll have to be prepared for excess. She formed her opinions in the very teeth of the storm, fighting in her family, and succeeded in establishing her personal life against great odds. Mirabai pushed her way out of her family, out of many social demands, and ignored many commands given to her as a woman of her time. Her religious passion carried her into intensities that make most people turn pale.

> I would like my own body to turn into a heap of incense and
>   sandalwood and you set a torch to it.
> When I've fallen down to gray ashes, smear me on your shoulders
>   and chest.

We know that hundreds of singers and dancers at that time participated in this sort of excess.

We could say that her poetry brings to us three huge illuminations. First, we get the feeling of what it's like to rebel against entrenched patriarchal interests and a deeply rooted social order. Also, we can sense through her poetry the power of the Krishna movement. Krishna was said to free Indian women from long-standing bonds, and in one story he makes love with a hundred married women at night in the river. Also, we can feel how much Mirabai's poems were like a moving fire—not so friendly to people of wealth, it is a fire from another world.

One has to admire the Indian religious culture for being able to sustain the challenge of such fierce speakers as Kabir, Tulsidas, and Mirabai. We recall that Margaret Porete spoke of similar passions, and she was burned to death in Paris in 1302. Mirabai sustained threats, but she did survive.

When a poem of Mirabai's flows freely, one feels a fast-moving river of thought going in channels of enormous depth, moving and twisting around rocks with quick intelligence. Her river of thought holds the delicate heart of ardor, loverhood, teacher-devotion, Isolde-like intensity, and then mingles that ecstasy with a steely Joan-of-Arc rebelliousness. Her refusal to adjust to a low-spirited social order is so firm and well backed that the order entrenched by men, priests, or angry aunts doesn't have a chance in hell of standing against her. Sarcasm is a fine weapon for her.

> I don't steal money, I don't hit anyone. What will you charge me
> with?

Krishna has the darker face of people in southern India, and she sometimes calls him the Dark One.

> My friend, I went to the market and bought the Dark One.
> You claim by night, I say by day.
> Actually I was beating a drum all the time I was buying him.
> You say I gave too much; I say too little.
> Actually I put him on a scale before I bought him.

Jane Hirshfield has set down some magnificent lines of Mirabai's about what will happen when you offer the Great One your life:

> Be ready to orbit his lamp like a moth giving in to the light,
> To live in the deer as she runs toward the hunter's call,
> In the partridge that swallows hot coals for love of the moon.

MIRABAI was born in Rajasthan in 1498, while the Hindu Rajputs were still resisting the Muslim domination; they kept their own dreams of family honor and military greatness. Thirty years after Mirabai's birth, the first great Mughal emperor invaded India and established the Mughal Dynasty at Delhi.

Among Rajputs, a family was a feudal patriarchy requiring battle courage in men, chastity and obedience in women.

Mira was born in the village of Kudki. It is said that when she was a tiny girl, she begged from a visiting ascetic a small statue of Krishna that he carried. She refused to eat or drink until she received it. Apparently the ascetic received a dream ordering him to give the statue to Mirabai.

In 1516, she married the son of the Rana Sangha, the leader of the Rajputs. This moment of her life has been decorated with many stories. People say that she insisted on being married to the statuette of Krishna before the marriage to her husband. The marriage did not last long; her husband died after only three years.

It is also said that she had a guru who was an Untouchable, living in the little town near the castle. Her family refused to allow her to make any contact with him, so she would tie her saris together and climb down the castle wall at night. She would wash his old feet with water and then drink it.

Her husband's family failed to control her and apparently tried to kill her several times. In one poem, she mentions the son of Rana Sangha sending her a cup of poison, and later a poisonous snake. She says in a song that she put it around her neck and thanked him for the jewelry. Sometime later, she left the castle and began to travel to Brindavan where Krishna had lived as a youth. Apparently she traveled widely around north India, singing and reciting poems, and arrived at last at the temple at Dwaraka. About 1546, when she would have been forty-eight, it seems a group of Brahmans went to her and staked out the temple, planning to starve to death in such a way that she would seem to be responsible for their death. About this time she wrote a song to Krishna that became a favorite of Mahatma Gandhi centuries later. We don't know when or how she died.

Many versions of her poems exist because different villages she visited kept the songs alive in their own way. Shama Futehally believes that about two hundred poems are authentic among the thousands extant. Most genuine poems exist in a medieval form of the Hindu dialect spoken in Braj. The last line ordinarily includes Mira's name as well as a mention of Krishna, sometimes in a metaphorical way such as The One Who Lifts Mountains. In our time, Subbalakshmi sings Mira's songs all over India, and they still feel fresh and contemporary.

The versions here were done with the help of the East Asian Language Department at the University of Chicago, which gave me originals and word-by-word translations prepared for students in the course on Mirabai.

THE HEAT OF MIDNIGHT TEARS

Listen, my friend, this road is the heart opening,
Kissing his feet, resistance broken, tears all night.

If we could reach the Lord through immersion in water,
I would have asked to be born a fish in this life.
If we could reach Him through nothing but berries and wild nuts,
Then surely the saints would have been monkeys when they came
    from the womb!
If we could reach him by munching lettuce and dry leaves,
Then the goats would surely get to the Holy One before us!

If the worship of stone statues could bring us all the way,
I would have adored a granite mountain years ago.

Mirabai says: The heat of midnight tears will bring you to God.

THE CLOUDS

When I saw the dark clouds, I wept, O Dark One, I wept at the dark
  clouds.
Black clouds soared up, and took some yellow along; rain did fall,
  some rain fell long.
There was water east of the house, west of the house; fields all green.
The one I love lives past those fields; rain has fallen on my body, on
  my hair, as I wait in the open door for him.
The Energy that holds up mountains is the energy Mirabai bows
  down to.
He lives century after century, and the test I set for him he has passed.

THE MUSIC

My friend, the stain of the Great Dancer has penetrated my body.
I drank the cup of music, and I am hopelessly drunk.
Moreover I stay drunk, no matter what I do to become sober.
Rana, who disapproves, gave me one basket with a snake in it.
Mira folded the snake around her neck, it was a lover's necklace, lovely!
Rana's next gift was poison: "This is something for you, Mira."
She repeated the Holy Name in her chest, and drank it, it was good!
Every name He has is praise; that's the cup I like to drink, and only
    that.
"The Great Dancer is my husband," Mira says, "rain washes off all the
    other colors."

DON'T GO, DON'T GO

Don't go, don't go. I touch your soles. I'm sold to you.

No one knows where to find the bhakti path, show me where to go.

I would like my own body to turn into a heap of incense and sandalwood and you set a torch to it.

When I've fallen down to gray ashes, smear me on your shoulders and chest.

Mira says: You who lift the mountains, I have some light, I want to mingle it with yours.

FAITHFULNESS

My friend, he looked, and our eyes met; an arrow came in.

My chest opened; what could it do? His image moved inside.

I've been standing all morning in the door of my house, looking down the road.

The one I love is dark: he is an herb growing in secret places, an herb that heals wounds.

Mira says: The town thinks I am loose, but I am faithful to the Dark One.

ALL I WAS DOING WAS BREATHING

Something has reached out and taken in the beams of my eyes.

There is a longing, it is for his body, for every hair of that dark body.

All I was doing was being, and the Dancing Energy came by my house.

His face looks curiously like the moon, I saw it from the side, smiling.

My family says: "Don't ever see him again!" And imply things in a low voice.

But my eyes have their own life; they laugh at rules, and know whose they are.

I believe I can bear on my shoulders whatever you want to say of me.

Mira says: Without the energy that lifts mountains, how am I to live?

IT'S TRUE I WENT TO THE MARKET

My friend, I went to the market and bought the Dark One.
You claim by night, I say by day.
Actually I was beating a drum all the time I was buying him.
You say I gave too much; I say too little.
Actually I put him on a scale before I bought him.
What I paid was my social body, my town body, my family body, and
    all my inherited jewels.
Mirabai says: The Dark One is my husband now.
Be with me when I lie down; you promised me this in an earlier life.

THE COFFER WITH THE
POISONOUS SNAKE

Rana sent a gold coffer of complicated ivory;
But inside a black and green asp was waiting,
"It is a necklace that belonged to a great Queen!"
I put it around my neck; it fit well.
It became a string of lovely pearls, each with a moon inside.
My room then was full of moonlight as if the full moon
Had found its way in through the open window.

WHERE DID YOU GO?

Where did you go, Holy One, after you left my body?
Your flame jumped to the wick, and then you disappeared and left the
   lamp alone.
You put the boat into the surf, and then walked inland, leaving the
   boat in the ocean of parting.
Mira says: Tell me when you will come to meet me.

ANKLE BELLS

Mira dances, how can her ankle bells not dance?
"Mira is insane," strangers say that, "the family's ruined."
Poison came to the door one day; she drank it and laughed.
I am at Hari's feet; I give him body and soul.
A glimpse of him is water: How thirsty I am for that!
Mira's Lord is the one who lifts mountains, he removes evil from
  human life.
Mira's Lord attacks the beings of greed; for safety I go to him.

HIS HAIR

You play the flute well; I love your swing curls and your earlocks.
Jasumati, your mother, wasn't she the one
Who washed and combed your beautiful hair?
If you come anywhere near my house,
I will close my sandalwood doors, and lock you in.

Mira's lord is half lion and half man.
She turns her life over to the midnight of his hair.

WHY MIRA CAN'T COME BACK
TO HER OLD HOUSE

The colors of the Dark One have penetrated Mira's body; all the other
   colors washed out.
Making love with the Dark One and eating little, those are my pearls
   and my carnelians.
Meditation beads and the forehead streak, those are my scarves and
   my rings.
That's enough feminine wiles for me. My teacher taught me this.
Approve me or disapprove me: I praise the Mountain Energy night
   and day.
I take the path that ecstatic human beings have taken for centuries.
I don't steal money, I don't hit anyone. What will you charge me
   with?
I have felt the swaying of the elephant's shoulders; and now you want
   me to climb on a jackass? Try to be serious.

KABIR

FOR THOSE WHO KNOW something of Indian spiritual literature, the word *Kabir* instantly calls up a razor-sharp intellect, an outrageous boldness in speech, inspired scolding of the fuzzy-minded:

> The idea that the soul will join with the ecstatic
> just because the body is rotten—
> that is all fantasy.
> What is found now is found then.
> If you find nothing now,
> you will simply end up with an apartment in the City of Death.

A young poet traveling with me made up a line as we passed through Chicago:

> If you find nothing now,
> you will simply end up with a suite in the Ramada Inn of death.

The change is proper. Kabir never used the elegant language of the Indian upper or middle classes; he wanted his metaphors to awaken the sleepers. His metaphors act like a loose electric wire, or a two-by-four to the head. His contempt for those wishing to be saved by being good is endless. In Kabir's poems, you see an astonishing event— highly religious and intensely spiritual poems written outside of, and in opposition to, the standard Hindu, Mohammedan, or Christian dogmas. Kabir says: "Suppose you scrub your ethical skin until it shines, but inside there is no music, then what?"

His poems are amazing, even from his broad culture, for the way they unite in one body the two traditions—ecstatic Sufism, which is supremely confident, a secretive, desert meditation, utterly opposed to orthodoxy and academics, and given to dancing and weeping—and the Hindu tradition, which is more sober on the surface, coming through the Vedas and Vishnu, Rama, and Krishna.

> Fire, air, earth, water and space—if you don't want the secret one,
>   you can't have these either.

> Kabir will tell you the truth; this is what love is like:
> suppose you had to cut your head off
> and give it to someone else,
> what difference would that make?

In the shortest of his poems, he models the high-spiritedness that he thought is essential for the life we live on this earth.

> The buds are shouting:
> "The Gardener is coming.
> Today he picks the blossoms,
> Tomorrow, us!"

If we cannot recite that last line with joy, then we are probably too gloomy to take Kabir in. He wants us not to worry whether we live or die.

Thought and feeling in most religious poets swim together. In Kabir one leaps ahead of the other, as if jumping out of the sea, and the reader smiles in joy at so much energy. It is as if both thought and feeling feed a third thing, a rebellious originality, and with that tail the poem shoots through the water. We feel that speed sometimes in

Eckhart also. Kabir says that interior work is not done by method, but by intensity. "Look at me, and you will see a slave of that intensity." The word "intensity" widens to its full range here, bringing in intense feeling, thinking, intuition, and intense love of colors and odors and animals. With our good ears, he says, we should hear the sound of "the anklets on the feet of an insect as it walks."

KABIR was born in perhaps 1398, probably into a class of weavers recently converted to Islam. One story of his childhood is told over and over. Ramananda, the Hindu master, would accept only Brahmans as disciples, and refused Kabir. Kabir knew that Ramananda went down the steps of the ghat before dawn every morning at Benares for a bath. In the half-dark, Kabir lay on one of the steps. Ramananda stepped on him and, startled, cried out, "Rama!" Kabir said, "You spoke the name of God in my presence; you initiated me. I am your student." Ramananda accepted him, and Kabir was with him for a long time.

He evidently worked as a weaver himself. He lived as a householder, and draws many images from householding or weaving. It is said that he was married, and that he fed every mendicant who came to his house.

Historically, Kabir's life is associated with the gradual rise of "bhakti energy" in India. In the Indian subcontinent, a vast rise of bhakti energy began in the eighth or ninth century A.D., as if ocean water had suddenly reappeared in the center of a continent. Sometime during those centuries, an alternative to the Vedic chanting began. Scholars knew the texts in Sanskrit, and the chanting of the Vedas was done by trained priests in what we might call "religious academics." The new bhakti worship involved the present tense, and contemporary language, more than the old "classical" tongue. Singing and dancing came forward—we see it in Mirabai's poems too—love of color, of intensity, of the male-female poles, of the avoidance of convention.

The poets of India began to write ecstatic poetry in their local languages, and thus refreshed the bhakti experience "from underneath." Some poems were written specifically for the long bhakti sessions, which lasted three or four hours in the middle of the night, and were guided through their stages by chanted and sung poems.

Kabir is thought to have died in Benares, and Bankey Behari estimates the year as 1527, when Kabir would have been 129 years old.

THE CLAY JUG

Inside this clay jug there are canyons and pine mountains, and the
    maker of canyons and pine mountains!
All seven oceans are inside, and hundreds of millions of stars.
The acid that tests gold is there, and the one who judges jewels.
And the music from the strings no one touches, and the source of all
    water.

If you want the truth, I will tell you the truth:
Friend, listen: the God whom I love is inside.

THE OWL AND THE MOON

Why should we two ever want to part?

Just as the leaf of the water rhubarb lives floating on the water,
we live as the great one and the little one.

As the owl opens his eyes all night to the moon,
we live as the great one and the little one.

This love between us goes back to the first humans;
it cannot *be* annihilated.

Here is Kabir's idea: as the river gives itself into the ocean,
what is inside me moves inside you.

THE THIRSTY FISH

I laugh when I hear that the fish in the water is thirsty.

You don't grasp the fact that what is most alive of all is inside your
    own house;
and so you walk from one holy city to the next with a confused look!

Kabir will tell you the truth: go wherever you like, to Calcutta
    or Tibet;
if you can't find where your soul is hidden,
for you the world will never be real!

WHAT MADE KABIR A SERVANT

Between the conscious and the unconscious, the mind has put up a
    swing;
all earth creatures, even the supernovas, sway between these two trees,
and it never winds down.

Angels, animals, humans, insects by the million, also the wheeling sun
    and moon;
ages go by, and it goes on.

Everything is swinging: heaven, earth, water, fire,
and the secret one slowly growing a body.
Kabir saw that for fifteen seconds, and it made him a servant for life.

THE MEETING

When my friend is away from me, I am depressed;
nothing in the daylight delights me,
sleep at night gives no rest,
who can I tell about this?

The night is dark, and long . . . hours go by . . .
because I am alone, I sit up suddenly,
fear goes through me. . . .

Kabir says: Listen, my friend
there is one thing in the world that satisfies,
and that is a meeting with the Guest.

THE ONLY WOMAN AWAKE

Friends, wake up! Why do you go on sleeping?
The night is over—do you want to lose the day the same way?
Other women who managed to get up early have already found an
    elephant or a jewel. . . .
So much was lost already while you slept . . .
and that was so unnecessary!

The one who loves you understood, but you did not.
You forgot to make a place in your bed next to you.
Instead you spent your life playing.
In your twenties you did not grow
because you did not know who your Lord was.
Wake up! Wake up! There's no one in your bed—
He left you during the long night.

Kabir says: The only woman awake is the woman who has heard the
    flute!

THE RADIANCE IN YOUR
MOTHER'S WOMB

I talk to my inner lover, and I say, why such rush?

We sense that there is some sort of spirit that loves birds and animals
and the ants—

perhaps the same one who gave a radiance to you in your mother's
womb.

Is it logical you would be walking around entirely orphaned now?

The truth is you turned away yourself,

and decided to go into the dark alone.

Now you are tangled up in others, and have forgotten what you once
knew,

and that's why everything you do has some weird failure in it.

THINK WHILE YOU ARE ALIVE

Friend, hope for the Guest while you are alive.
Jump into experience while you are alive!
Think . . . and think . . . while you are alive.
What you call "salvation" belongs to the time before death.

If you don't break your ropes while you're alive,
do you think
ghosts will do it after?

The idea that the soul will join with the ecstatic
just because the body is rotten—
that is all fantasy.
What is found now is found then.
If you find nothing now,
you will simply end up with an apartment in the City of Death.
If you make love with the divine now, in the next life you will have the
    face of satisfied desire.
So plunge into the truth, find out who the Teacher is, believe in the
    Great Sound!
Kabir says this: When the Guest is being searched for, it is the intensity
    of the longing for the Guest that does all the work.
Look at me, and you will see a slave of that intensity.

THE LAMP WITHOUT OIL

I know the sound of the ecstatic flute,
but I don't know whose flute it is.

A lamp burns and has neither wick nor oil.

A lily pad blossoms and is not attached to the bottom!

When one flower opens, ordinarily dozens open.

The moon bird's head is filled with nothing but thoughts of the
  moon,
and when the next rain will come is all that the rain bird thinks of.

Who is it we spend our entire life loving?

THE SPIRITUAL ATHLETE IN
AN ORANGE ROBE

The spiritual athlete often changes the color of his clothes,
and his mind remains gray and loveless.

He sits inside a shrine room all day,
so that God has to go outdoors and praise the rocks.

Or he drills holes in his ears, his beard grows enormous and matted,
people mistake him for a goat. . . .
He goes out into wilderness areas, strangles his impulses,
and makes himself neither male nor female. . . .

He shaves his skull, puts his robe in an orange vat,
reads the Bhagavad Gita, and becomes a terrific talker.

Kabir says: Actually you are going in a hearse to the country of death,
bound hand and foot!

ARE YOU LOOKING FOR ME?

Are you looking for me? I am in the next seat.
My shoulder is against yours.
You will not find me in stupas, not in Indian shrine rooms, nor in
    synagogues, nor in cathedrals:
not in masses, nor kirtans, not in legs winding around your own neck,
    nor in eating nothing but vegetables.
When you really look for me, you will see me instantly—
you will find me in the tiniest house of time.
Kabir says: Student, tell me, what is God?
He is the breath inside the breath.

THE HOLY POOLS HAVE ONLY WATER

There is nothing but water in the holy pools.
I know, I have been swimming in them.
All the gods sculpted of wood and ivory can't say a word.
I know, I have been crying out to them.
The Sacred Books of the East are nothing but words.
I looked through their covers one day sideways.
What Kabir talks of is only what he has lived through.
If you have not lived through something, it is not true.

WHY ARRANGE THE PILLOWS

Oh friend, I love you, think this over
carefully! If you are in love,
then why are you asleep?

If you have found him,
give yourself to him, take him.

Why do you lose track of him again and again?

If you are about to fall into heavy sleep anyway,
why waste time smoothing the bed
and arranging the pillows?

Kabir will tell you the truth; this is what love is like:
suppose you had to cut your head off
and give it to someone else,
what difference would that make?

MY FIRST MARRIAGE

I married my Lord, and meant to live with him.
But I did not live with him, I turned away,
and all at once my twenties were gone.

The night I was married, all my friends sang for me,
and the rice of pleasure and the rice of pain fell on me.

Yet when all those ceremonies were over, I left, I did not go home
    with him,
and my relatives all the way home said, "It's all right."

Kabir says: Now my love energy is actually mine.
This time I will take it with me when I go,
and outside his house I will blow the horn of triumph!

THE MUSIC WITHOUT STRINGS

Have you heard the music that no fingers enter into?
Far inside the house
entangled music—
What is the sense of leaving your house?

Suppose you scrub your ethical skin until it shines,
but inside there is no music,
then what?

Mohammed's son pores over words, and points out this
and that,
but if his chest is not soaked dark with love,
then what?

The Yogi comes along in his famous orange.
But if inside he is colorless, then what?

Kabir says: Every instant that the sun is risen, if I stand in the temple,
   or on a balcony, in the hot fields, or in a walled garden, my own
   Lord is making love with me.

ANTONIO MACHADO

ANTONIO MACHADO WRITES poems that seem, after we know them well, to be words written by a close friend. There is a hidden "we" in his poems:

> Last night, as I was sleeping,
> I dreamt—marvellous error!—
> that I had a beehive
> here inside my heart.
> And the golden bees
> were making white combs
> and sweet honey
> from my old failures.

It doesn't feel confessional; it's not a complaint; we don't sense the self-obsession of so many confessional poems. He dreams that bees were making white combs and sweet honey from his old failures. The image is calm and matter-of-fact, and no one else seems to be able to do that.

So many readers have written to me saying that this poem is the first poem they'd ever memorized.

The important year for Machado and his generation was 1898, the year of the Spanish-American War, when Spain lost the rest of her empire. Machado was twenty-three. It seems clear that the old rhetorical lies of the politicians and the Church had finally come to nothing. It was over. The whole elaborate business of empire had collapsed, and the young ones now had to live with reduced expectations, some sadness and grief. It amounted to a new start in poetry, using a few words that were honest.

> It's possible that while we were dreaming
> the hand that casts out the stars like seeds
> started up the ancient music once more

> —like a note from a great harp—
> and the frail wave came to our lips
> in the form of one or two honest words.

The time for lectures is over. How do we cross over the space between us and another person?

> To talk with someone,
> ask a question first,
> then—listen.

Machado said that if we pay attention exclusively to the inner world, it will dissolve; if we pay attention exclusively to the outer world, it will dissolve. To create art, we have to stitch together both the inner and the outer worlds. How to do that? Machado concludes, Well, we could always use our eyes.

One of his earliest memories, which he published among his notebooks, was this: "I'd like to tell you the most important thing that ever happened to me. One day when I was still quite young, my mother and I went out walking. I had a piece of sugar cane in my hand, I remember—it was in Seville, in some vanished Christmas season. Just ahead of us were another mother and child—he had a stick of sugar cane too. I was sure mine was bigger—I knew it was! Even so, I asked my mother—because children always ask questions they already know the answer to: 'Mine's bigger, isn't it?' And she said, 'No, my boy, it's not. What have you done with your eyes?' I've been asking myself that question ever since."

ANTONIO MACHADO was born on July 26, 1875, in Seville. His father was a teacher and early collector of folk poetry and folk music in Spain. When Antonio was eight, the family moved to Madrid; there Antonio and his brothers attended the Free Institution of Learning, whose founder, Francisco Giner de los Ríos, had a profound effect on two or three generations of Spanish intellectuals and writers. Antonio tended to be torpid and slow; he took ten extra years to get his B.A. Eventually he chose a career as a secondary-school teacher of French, passed the examination, and, when he was thirty-two, got his first job at Soria, a poor and exhausted town in the grazed-out mountain area of Castile. He stayed there five years. During the second year he married the daughter of the family in whose pension he lived, Leonor, then fifteen. They went to Paris for work at the Sorbonne; they lived in poor quarters; she caught tuberculosis and died two years later, in the fall of 1911. "She is always with me," he said; he often addressed her in later poems, and never remarried. He resigned his position at Soria, and transferred to Baeza, in the south, where he stayed seven years. During 1912, his last year in Soria, his second book, *The Countryside of Castile,* came out; and he continued to add poems to it during his years in Baeza. In 1919, he transferred again, this time to Segovia, which is only an hour from Madrid. He was now able to escape on weekends from provincial life, which he complained was boring and deadening; and he began writing plays and taking part in the intellectual life of Madrid. He lived in Segovia from 1919 to 1932, thirteen years, during which time he fell in love with a married woman he called "Guiomar," invented two poet-philosophers named Abel Martín and Juan de Mairena, and published his third book, *Nuevas Canciones (New Poems).* He became more and more active in public life, writing in the papers on political and moral issues during the tense period that led in 1931 to the proclamation of the Second Spanish Republic. He moved to Madrid in 1932 and took a strong part in the defense of the Republic. The civil war began in 1936. Finally, in late January of 1939, moving ahead of Franco's army, he crossed the Pyrenees. In the last picture we have of Antonio, he is a passenger in an old Ford—his manuscripts all lost—holding his mother on his lap, entering France. He died at Collioure, just over the border, on February 22, 1939, and as the gravestones, which I saw, make clear, his mother survived him by only a few days.

MEMORY FROM CHILDHOOD

A chilly and overcast afternoon
of winter. The students
are studying. Steady boredom
of raindrops across the windowpanes.

Recess over. In a poster
Cain is shown running
away, and Abel dead,
not far from a red spot.

The teacher, with a voice husky and hollow,
is thundering. He is an old man badly dressed,
withered and dried up,
holding a book in his hand.

And the whole children's choir
is singing its lesson:
"one thousand times one hundred is one hundred thousand,
one thousand times one thousand is one million."

A chilly and overcast afternoon
of winter. The students
are studying. Steady boredom
of raindrops across the windowpanes.

THE CLOCK STRUCK TWELVE TIMES

The clock struck twelve times . . . and it was a spade
knocked twelve times against the earth.
. . . "It's my turn!" I cried. . . . The silence
answered me: Do not be afraid.
You will never see the last drop fall
that now is trembling in the water clock.

You will still sleep many hours
here on the beach,
and one clear morning you will find
your boat tied to another shore.

CLOSE TO THE ROAD

Close to the road, we sit down one day.
Now our life amounts to time, and our sole concern
the attitudes of despair we adopt
while we wait. But She will not fail to arrive.

THE WATER WHEEL

The afternoon arrived
mournful and dusty.

The water was composing
its countrified poem
in the buckets
of the lazy water wheel.

The mule was dreaming—
old and sad mule!
in time to the darkness
that was talking in the water.

The afternoon arrived
mournful and dusty.

I don't know which noble
and religious poet
joined the anguish
of the endless wheel

to the cheerful music
of the dreaming water,
and bandaged your eyes—
old and sad mule! . . .

But it must have been a noble
and religious poet,
a heart made mature
by darkness and art.

LAST NIGHT, AS I WAS SLEEPING

Last night, as I was sleeping,
I dreamt—marvellous error!—
that a spring was breaking
out in my heart.
I said: Along which secret aqueduct,
Oh water, are you coming to me,
water of a new life
that I have never drunk?

Last night, as I was sleeping,
I dreamt—marvellous error!—
that I had a beehive
here inside my heart.
And the golden bees
were making white combs
and sweet honey
from my old failures.

Last night, as I was sleeping,
I dreamt—marvellous error!—
that a fiery sun was giving
light inside my heart.
It was fiery because I felt
warmth as from a hearth,
and sun because it gave light
and brought tears to my eyes.

Last night, as I slept,
I dreamt—marvellous error!—
that it was God I had
here inside my heart.

IS MY SOUL ASLEEP?

Is my soul asleep?
Have those beehives that labor
at night stopped? And the water
wheel of thought,
is it dry, the cups empty,
wheeling, carrying only shadows?

No my soul is not asleep.
It is awake, wide awake.
It neither sleeps nor dreams, but watches,
its clear eyes open,
far-off things, and listens
at the shores of the great silence.

FROM THE DOORSILL OF A DREAM

From the doorsill of a dream they called my name . . .
It was the good voice, the voice I loved so much.

"Listen: Will you go with me to visit the soul? . . ."
A soft stroke reached up to my heart.

"With you, always . . ." And in my dream I walked
down a long and solitary corridor,
aware of the touching of the pure robe
and the soft beating of blood in the hand that loved me.

THE WIND, ONE BRILLIANT DAY

The wind, one brilliant day, called
to my soul with an aroma of jasmine.

"In return for the odor of my jasmine,
I'd like all the odor of your roses."

"I have no roses; all the flowers
in my garden are dead."

"Well then, I'll take the waters of the fountains,
and the withered petals and the yellow leaves."

The wind left. And I wept. And I said to myself:
"What have you done with the garden that was entrusted to you?"

IT'S POSSIBLE THAT WHILE WE WERE DREAMING

It's possible that while we were dreaming
the hand that casts out the stars like seeds
started up the ancient music once more

—like a note from a great harp—
and the frail wave came to our lips
in the form of one or two honest words.

PORTRAIT

My childhood is memories of a patio in Seville,
and a garden where sunlit lemons are growing yellow;
my youth twenty years on the earth of Castile;
what I lived a few things you'll forgive me for omitting.

A great seducer I was not, nor the lover of Juliet;
—the oafish way I dress is enough to say that—
but the arrow Cupid planned for me I got,
and I loved whenever women found a home in me.

A flow of leftist blood moves through my body,
but my poems rise from a calm and deep spring.
There is a man of rule who behaves as he should, but more
than him, I am, in the good sense of the word, good.

I adore beauty, and following contemporary thought
have cut some old roses from the garden of Ronsard;
but the new lotions and feathers are not for me;
I am not one of the blue jays who sing so well.

I dislike hollow tenors who warble of love,
and the chorus of crickets singing to the moon.
I fall silent so as to separate voices from echoes,
and I listen among the voices to one voice and only one.

Am I classic or Romantic? Who knows. I want to leave
my poetry as a fighter leaves his sword, known
for the masculine hand that closed around it,
not for the coded mark of the proud forger.

I talk always to the man who walks along with me;
—men who talk to themselves hope to talk to God someday—
My soliloquies amount to discussions with this friend,
who taught me the secret of loving human beings.

In the end, I owe you nothing; you owe me what I've written.
I turn to my work; with what I've earned I pay
for my clothes and hat, the house in which I live,
the food that feeds my body, the bed on which I sleep.

And when the day arrives for the last leaving of all,
and the ship that never returns to port is ready to go,
you'll find me on board, light, with few belongings,
almost naked like the children of the sea.

POEMS CHOSEN FROM
MORAL PROVERBS AND FOLK SONGS

(*The Countryside of Castile*)

1

I love Jesus, who said to us:
Heaven and earth will pass away.
When heaven and earth have passed away,
my word will remain.
What was your word, Jesus?
Love? Affection? Forgiveness?
All your words were
one word: Wakeup.

2

It is good knowing that glasses
are to drink from;
the bad thing is not to know
what thirst is for.

3

You say nothing is created new?
Don't worry about it, with the mud
of the earth, make a cup
from which your brother can drink.

4

All things die and all things live forever;
but our task is to die,
to die making roads,
roads over the sea.

5

    To die . . . To fall like a drop
of water into the big ocean?
Or to be what I've never been:
a man without a shadow, without a dream,
a man all alone, walking,
without a mirror, and with no road?

6

    Mankind owns four things
that are no good at sea:
rudder, anchor, oars,
and the fear of going down.

RAINBOW AT NIGHT

for Don Ramón del Valle-Inclán

The train moves through the Guadarrama
one night on the way to Madrid.
The moon and the fog create
high up a rainbow.
Oh April moon, so calm,
driving the white clouds!

The mother holds her boy
sleeping on her lap.
The boy sleeps, and nevertheless
sees the green fields outside,
and trees lit up by sun,
and the golden butterflies.

The mother, her forehead dark
between a day gone and a day to come,
sees a fire nearly out
and an oven with spiders.

There's a traveler mad with grief,
no doubt seeing odd things;
he talks to himself, and when he looks
wipes us out with his look.

I remember fields under snow,
and pine trees of other mountains.

And you, Lord, through whom we all
have eyes, and who sees souls,
tell us if we all one
day will see your face.

FOURTEEN POEMS CHOSEN FROM
MORAL PROVERBS AND FOLK SONGS
(*Nuevas Canciones*)

Dedicated to José Ortega y Gasset

1

The eye you see is not
an eye because you see it;
it is an eye because it sees you.

2

To talk with someone,
ask a question first,
then — listen.

3

Narcissism
is an ugly fault,
and now it's a boring fault too.

4

But look in your mirror for the other one,
the other one who walks by your side.

5

Between living and dreaming
there is a third thing.
Guess it.

6

Look for your other half
who walks always next to you
and tends to be what you aren't.

7

In my solitude
I have seen things very clearly
that were not true.

8

Form your letters slowly and well:
making things well
is more important than making them.

9

What the poet is searching for
is not the fundamental I
but the deep you.

10

Beyond living and dreaming
there is something more important:
waking up.

11

Pay attention now:
a heart that's all by itself
is not a heart.

12

If it's good to live,
then it's better to be asleep dreaming,
and best of all,
mother, is to awake.

13

When I am alone
how close my friends are;
when I am with them
how distant they are!

14

But art?
It is pure and intense play,
so it is like pure and intense life,
so it is like pure and intense fire.
You'll see the coal burning.

TODAY'S MEDITATION

The fiery palm tree in front of me,
that the setting sun is just now leaving,
this late and silent afternoon,
inside our peaceful garden,
while flowery old Valencia
drinks the Guadalaviar waters —
Valencia of delicate towers,
in the joyful sky of Ausias March,
her river turns entirely into roses
before it arrives at the sea —
I think of the war. The war
is like a tornado moving
through the bleak foothills of the Duero,
through the plains of standing wheat,
from the farmlands of Extremadura
to these gardens with private lemons,
from the gray skies of the north
to these salty marshes full of light.
I think of Spain, all of it sold out,
river by river, mountain by mountain, sea to sea.

JUAN RAMÓN JIMÉNEZ

JIMÉNEZ, ALONG WITH Antonio Machado and Unamuno, led the great and joyful revival of Spanish poetry in the years around 1910. They all dreamed of a new blossoming of Spain. Jiménez was not robust. He was delicate, and slipped off into the sanitorium more than once. Yet his devotion to poetry was healthy and rigorous. He spent years editing poetry magazines and starting publishing ventures to get poets in print, spending endless afternoons poring over young poets' manuscripts. His delight and Machado's stubbornness prepared the way for the great generation of '28: Lorca, Aleixandre, Salinas, Guillén. Lorca's early poems are imitations of Juan Ramón's, who had thrown up light and airy houses made out of willows, and in so many different designs, that all the coming Spanish poets found themselves living in one or another of his willow houses before they moved into their own houses.

He said that poetry is the highest form of speech. Its essence was an inner subtle life; Jiménez added a fierce devotion to craft. "Written poetry continues to seem to me as a form of expression, of that which cannot be said." He asked what sort of life we should have to feel the most poetry. He needed solitude, some distance. When people called at his house, he could reply, "Juan Ramón Jiménez is not home today." Yet his warmth is what first drew people to him. In 1903, he wrote a review praising *Soledades,* the first book of Antonio Machado. His book of prose poems in which he talks to a donkey (*Platero y yo,*— "Platero and Myself," 1917) was immensely popular and is still a book of love to Andalusia.

In 1916, he took a trip to New York, to marry Zenobia Camprubi, whose brother owned a Spanish-language newspaper in New York. His book of poems about that trip, called *Diary of a Poet Recently Married,* is a masterpiece. It includes marvelous prose poems about New York: describing his visit to Whitman's tiny house on Long Island, and about an hour he spent in the Author's Club (which he dreamed of burning down; the club was a hangout of third-rate writers in New York). He took a trip to Boston to admire the lavender windowpanes on Beacon Hill.

He kept changing his poetry toward new styles. He often referred to poetry as a woman. He summed up the whole tale of those changes once in a poem beginning: "At first she came to me pure." He loved the innocence of his early poetry. Then his poems, he said, began to pick up display, ostentation, and affectation, and he began to hate her. After a while, his poetry began to go back toward naiveté, candor, and plainspeaking. She was innocent again, and he fell in love once more. Finally, the poems became severe and naked: "Naked poetry, that I have loved my whole life!"

JUAN RAMÓN JIMÉNEZ was born in 1881 at Moguer in southern Andalusia. From his small town he sent his first poems to newspapers in Seville, and the writers there recognized his talent, and magazines in Madrid published his poetry. He received a letter of invitation signed by several writers, and in 1900, when he was eighteen, he arrived in Madrid to take part in Spanish literary life.

He began publishing books of poetry, and in 1906 started a review, *Renacimiento,* to celebrate the new Spanish poetry. In 1905, he returned to Moguer for seven years. He started then on his astonishing book of prose poems, *Platero y yo.*

When back in Madrid, he and his wife translated the complete works of Rabindranath Tagore, and he continued to work with young poets. He published *Estudiantes,* written in octosyllabic verse. He studied the

English poets, and translated Yeats, while continuing to publish new books of poetry.

In 1936, the Spanish Civil War began. He would have nothing to do with Franco, and went into exile. By the time the Spanish Civil War was over, Lorca was dead; Rafael Alberti, Jorge Guillén, Pedro Salinas, Emilio Prados, Manuel Altolaguirre, and Luis Cernuda were in exile.

Juan Ramón came first to the United States, living in Chevy Chase, Maryland, for a while. But the American literary community ignored him. He then moved to Puerto Rico, where he taught at the University of Puerto Rico until his death.

His love for his wife was one of the greatest devotions of his life, and he wrote many of his poems for her. When he received the Nobel Prize in 1956, his wife was on her deathbed; he told reporters to go away, that he would not go to Stockholm, that his wife should have been given the Nobel Prize, and he was not interested in receiving it. After his wife died, he did not write another poem and died a few months later, in the spring of 1958.

ADOLESCENCE

We were alone together
a moment on the balcony.
Since the lovely morning
of that day, we were sweethearts.

—The drowsy land around
was sleeping its vague colors,
under the gray and rosy
sunset of fall.

I told her I was going to kiss her;
she lowered her eyes calmly
and offered her cheeks to me
like someone losing a treasure.

—The dead leaves were falling
in the windless garden of the house,
and a perfume of heliotrope
was still floating in the air.

She did not dare to look at me;
I told her we would be married,
—and the tears rolled
from her mournful eyes.

FULL MOON

    The door is open,
the cricket is singing.
Are you going around naked
in the fields?

    Like an immortal water,
going in and out of everything.
Are you going around naked
in the air?

    The basil is not asleep,
the ant is busy.
Are you going around naked
in the house?

THE LUMBER WAGONS

The lumber wagons are already there.
—The pines and the wind have told us,
the golden moon has told us,
the smoke and the echo have told us . . .
They are the carts that go by
in these afternoons at dusk,
the lumber wagons carrying
the dead trees down from the mountain.
      What a sound of crying from these carts
on the road to Pueblo Nuevo!
      The oxen come along
in the starlight, daydreaming
about their warm stalls in the barn
smelling of motherhood and hay.
And behind the lumber wagons
the ox drivers walking,
the ox prod on their shoulders,
and eyes watching the sky.
      What a sound of crying from these carts
on the road to Pueblo Nuevo!
      The dead trees as they move
through the calm of the fields
leave behind a fresh honest smell
like a heart thrown open.
The Angelus falls
from the steeple of the ancient town
over the stripped fields
which smell like a cemetery.
      What a sound of crying from these carts
on the road to Pueblo Nuevo!

WHO KNOWS WHAT IS GOING ON

Who knows what is going on on the other side of each hour?

How many times the sunrise was
there, behind a mountain!

How many times the brilliant cloud piling up far off
was already a golden body full of thunder!

This rose was poison.

That sword gave life.

I was thinking of a flowery meadow
at the end of a road,
and found myself in the slough.

I was thinking of the greatness of what was human,
and found myself in the divine.

THE LAMB WAS BLEATING SOFTLY

The lamb was bleating softly.
The young jackass grew happier
with his excited bray.
The dog barked,
almost talking to the stars.
I woke up! I went out. I saw the tracks
of the sky on the ground
which had flowered
like a sky
turned upside down.
A warm and mild haze
hung around the trees;
the moon was going down
in a west of gold and silk
like some full and divine womb . . .
My chest was thumping
as if my heart were drunk . . .
I opened the barn door to see if
He was there.
He was!

"I TOOK OFF PETAL AFTER PETAL"

Birkendene, Caldwell,
    February 20

I took off petal after petal, as if you were a rose,
in order to see your soul,
and I didn't see it.

However, everything around—
horizons of fields and oceans—
everything, even what was infinite,
was filled with a perfume,
immense and living.

NIGHT PIECE

    The ship, slow and rushing at the same time, can get ahead of
     the water
but not the sky.
The blue is left behind, opened up in living silver,
and is ahead of us again.
The mast, fixed, swings and constantly returns
—like an hour hand that points
always to the same hour—
to the same stars,
hour after hour black and blue.
The body as it daydreams goes
toward the earth that belongs to it, from the other earth
that does not. The soul stays on board, moving
through the kingdom it has owned from birth.

WALT WHITMAN

"But do you really want to see Whitman's house instead of Roosevelt's? I've never had this request before!"

The house is tiny and yellow, and next to the railroad track, like the hut of a switchman, in a small green patch of grass, marked out with whitewashed stones, beneath a single tree. Around it, the wide meadow area is open to the wind, which sweeps it, and us, and has polished the simple rough piece of marble which announces to the trains:

TO MARK THE BIRTHPLACE OF
WALT WHITMAN
THE GOOD GRAY POET
BORN MAY 31, 1819
ERECTED BY THE COLONIAL SOCIETY
OF HUNTINGTON IN 1905

Since the farmer doesn't seem to be at home, I walk around the house a couple of times, hoping to see something through the windowlets. Suddenly a man, tall, slow-moving, and bearded, wearing a shirt and a wide-brimmed hat—like the early photograph of Whitman—comes, from somewhere, and tells me, leaning on his iron bar, that he doesn't know who Whitman was, that he is Polish, that this house is his, and that he does not intend to show it to anyone. Then pulling himself up, he goes inside, through the little door that looks like a toy door.

Solitude and cold. A train goes by, into the wind. The sun, scarlet for an instant, dies behind the low woods, and in the swamp we walk past, which is green and faintly blood-colored, innumerable toads are croaking in the enormous silence.

AUTHOR'S CLUB

I had always thought perhaps there would be no poets at all in New York. What I had never suspected was that there would be so many bad ones, or a place like this, as dry and dusty as our own Ateneo in Madrid, in spite of its being on the fifteenth floor, almost at the altitude of Parnassus.

Tenth-rate men, all of them, cultivating physical resemblances to Poe, to Walt Whitman, to Stevenson, to Mark Twain, letting their soul be burned up with their free cigar, since the two are the same: bushy-haired men who make fun of Robinson, Frost, Masters, Vachel Lindsay, Amy Lowell and who fail to make fun of Poe, Emily Dickinson, and Whitman only because they are already dead. And they show me wall after wall of portraits and autographs in holograph, of Bryant, of Aldrich, of Lowell, etc., etc., etc . . .

. . . I have taken a cigarette from the fumidor, lighted it, and thrown it into a corner, on the rug, in order to see if the fire will catch and leave behind it, in place of this club of rubbish, a high and empty hole, fresh and deep, with clear stars, in the cloudless sky of this April night.

LAVENDER WINDOWPANES AND
WHITE CURTAINS

Lavender windowpanes! They are like a pedigree of nobility. Boston has many of them and New York has a few, in the old streets around Washington Square, so pleasing, so hospitable, so full of silence! These beautiful panes survive particularly in Boston and are cared for with a haughty, self-interested zeal.

They go back to colonial days. The panes were made with substances which the sunlight over the years has been turning the color of the amethyst, of pansies, of the violet. One feels sure that between the sweet white muslin curtains of those quiet houses, he could glimpse through the violet pane the frail and noble spirit of those days, days of genuine silver and genuine gold, making no hearable sound.

Some of the panes have their violet color almost invisibly, like the flowers and stones I spoke of, and it takes skill simply to see it; others transfer their vague shading to their sister curtains, when the light of the pure sunsets strikes them; finally, by now a few panes are lavender all through, rotten with nobility.

My heart lingers back there with these panes, America, like an amethyst, a pansy, a violet, in the center of the muslin snow. I have been planting that heart for you in the ground beneath the magnolias that the panes reflect, so that each April the pink and white flowers and their odor will surprise the simple puritan women with their plain clothes, their noble look, and their pale gold hair, coming back at evening, quietly returning to their homes here in those calm spring hours that have made them homesick for earth.

OCEANS

    I have a feeling that my boat
has struck, down there in the depths,
against a great thing.
                And nothing
happens! Nothing . . . Silence . . . Waves . . .

    —Nothing happens? Or has everything happened,
and are we standing now, quietly, in the new life?

MUSIC

Music—
a naked woman
running mad through the pure night!

ROAD

They are all asleep, below.
                              Above, awake,
the helmsman and I.

He, watching the compass needle, lord
of the bodies, with their keys turned
in the locks. I, with my eyes
toward the infinite, guiding
the open treasures of the souls.

I AM NOT I

    I am not I.
              I am this one
walking beside me whom I do not see,
whom at times I manage to visit,
and whom at other times I forget;
the one who remains silent while I talk,
the one who forgives, sweet, when I hate,
the one who takes a walk when I am indoors,
the one who will remain standing when I die.

AT FIRST SHE CAME TO ME PURE

At first she came to me pure,
dressed only in her innocence;
and I loved her as we love a child.

Then she began putting on
clothes she picked up somewhere;
and I hated her, without knowing it.

She gradually became a queen,
the jewelry was blinding . . .
What bitterness and rage!

. . . She started going back toward nakedness.
And I smiled.

Soon she was back to the single shift
of her old innocence.
I believed in her a second time.

Then she took off the cloth
and was entirely naked . . .

Naked poetry, always mine,
that I have loved my whole life!

FRANCIS PONGE

FRANCIS PONGE is one of the wittiest poets who has ever lived. He is fond of prose poems, and his are unlike anyone else's. He leaps out of the wooden chest of French political verse and academic poetry and, adopting all of the rhetorical power of traditional French prose, begins pointing to objects such as a clump of blackberries, a closed oyster, a dinner plate, a tree losing its leaves in fall. He is the inventor of what we call these days the "thing" poem.

The intense eyes of Daumier have found their way into poetry. About a candle, he says: "Night at times revives a curious plant whose light makes powerfully furnished rooms fall apart into clumps of shadow." The candle "urges the reader on—then bends over onto its plate and drowns in what has always fed it." If the reader wants to extend this tiny metaphor into philosophy or religion, that is his job; the poet's job is finished.

About a frog, he says:

When rain like metal tips bounces off the sodden pastures, an amphibious dwarf, an Ophelia with empty sleeves, barely as large as a fist, rises at times from around the poet's feet, and then hurtles herself into the nearest pool.

You'll notice the Greek-based word "amphibious" and the Shakespearean-based "Ophelia" and the common French word for "fist" all brought together in a garden of leafy, grubby, colorful language plants. Even in translation, we can notice acute attention to the history of language. Ponge once said that he doesn't believe in the unconscious. He doesn't study it. Whatever is hidden you can already find in a French dictionary, looking at the history of a given word. If he is in trouble, he's liable to consult a dictionary the way someone else would consult a therapist.

When he turns to the oyster, he notices that the blows that a hungry person gave it leave whitish rings on the shell, "halos of some kind." Once inside, we see a "firmament with the upper heavens approaching the lower heavens." One will find also "a fringe of blackish lace." The pearl itself—should a pearl be present—is called a "beautiful expression." The oyster too is a writer.

And a door! Why not write a poem about a door? Opening it means "holding a door in our arms." Such pleasures that we rarely notice! "The pleasure of grabbing one of those tall barriers to a room abdominally, by its porcelain knot." The door has porcelain at its abdomen. And typically the labor we've gone through with the door moves toward privacy and secrecy as we close it again . . . "which the click of the powerful but well-oiled spring pleasantly confirms."

Many of our enthusiastic prose-poem composers haven't yet learned that the essence of the prose poem is not the absence of lines but the presence of wit.

One of Ponge's masterpieces is his poem about the ordinary dinner plate. The poem is elegant, and yet there are jokes every two seconds. He says: "No poetic leap, no matter how brilliant, can speak in a sufficiently flat way about the lowly interval that porcelain occupies between pure spirit and appetite."

Consulting his French dictionary, he then finds that *porcellana* in Latin means "sow vulva." "Is that good enough for your appetite?"

The plate finds itself compared to Aphrodite, who rose from the sea; suddenly it becomes a round sun; then many plates, all being "multiplied by that free-spirited juggler in the wings," who, as in the circus, replaces "the melancholic old man" who can offer us only one sun per day. The "melancholic old man" is apparently some kind of Jehovah.

FRANCIS PONGE was born in 1899 in Montpellier. As a young man, he moved to Paris. His first book, *Le Parti Pri des Choses*, or *The Side Taken by Things*, was begun around 1922, and he worked on it for close to twenty years before its publication in 1942. Camus came upon the book and wrote a long letter to Ponge. Camus showed the book to Sartre. It was Jean-Paul Sartre who called attention to Ponge's work in a major way. In 1942, Ponge joined the French Resistance and was part of it until the defeat of the Nazis. In ordinary life, he worked at various editorial and teaching jobs. He was a friend of many surrealist poets and painters, particularly Breton, Eluard, Giacometti, and Picasso. In his work, he looked back to Lucretius and Cicero and to the sixteenth-century Malherbe. In 1966, Ponge was a visiting professor at both Barnard College and Columbia University. He was awarded the Neustadt International Prize for Literature in 1974. He died in Paris in 1988.

TREES LOSE PARTS OF THEMSELVES INSIDE A CIRCLE OF FOG

Inside the fog that encloses the trees, they undergo a stripping. . . . Thrown into confusion by a slow oxidation, and humiliated by the sap's withdrawal for the sake of the flowers and fruits, the leaves, following the hot spells of August, cling less anyway.

The up-and-down tunnels inside the bark deepen, and guide the moisture down to earth so as to break off with the more animated parts of the tree.

The flowers are scattered, the fruits brought down. This giving up of their more animated parts, and even of parts of their body, has become, since their earliest days, a familiar pattern for trees.

THE FROG

When rain like metal tips bounces off the sodden pastures, an amphibious dwarf, an Ophelia with empty sleeves, barely as large as a fist, rises at times from around the poet's feet, and then hurtles herself into the nearest pool.

Let this nervous one flee. How beautiful her legs are. A glove impermeable to water envelops her body. Barely flesh at all, her long muscles in their elegance are neither animal nor fish. In order to escape from my fingers, the virtue of fluid allies in her with the battle of the life force. She puffs, widely goitered. . . . And this heart that beats so strongly, the wrinkly eyelids, the old woman's mouth, move me to set her free.

THE END OF FALL

What fall amounts to is really a cold infusion. The dead leaves of all herb species steep in the rain. But no fermenting goes on, no alcohol-making: one has to wait until spring to see the effect a compress has when applied to a wooden leg.

The counting of votes goes on chaotically. All the doors of the polling places fly open and slam shut. Into the wastebasket! Into the wastebasket! Nature rips up her manuscripts, tears down her library, knocks down the last fruits with long poles.

Then she rises crisply from her worktable. Her height all at once seems unusual. Her hair undone, she has her head in the fog. Arms loose, she breathes in with ecstasy the icy wind that makes all her ideas clear. The days are short, the night falls swiftly, who needs comedy.

Earth floating among the other planets regains her serious look. Her sunlit side is narrower, invaded by clefts of shadow. Her shoes, like a hobo's, are great with water, and a source of music.

Inside this frogpond, or energetic amphibiguity, everything regains strength, hops from stone to stone, tries a new field. Streams increase.

Here you see what is called a real soaking, a cleaning that cares nothing for respectability! Dressed as a naked man, soaked to the bone.

And it goes on, doesn't get dry right away. Three months of healthy reflecting goes on in this state; without any circulatory disaster, without bathrobe, without horsehair glove. But her strong constitution can take it.

And so, when the tiny buds begin to point, they know what they are doing and what is going on—and if they come out hesitatingly, numb and flushed, it is in full knowledge of why.

Ah well, but there hangs another tale—that may follow from, but certainly doesn't have the smell of, the black wooden ruler which I will now use to draw my line under this present story.

THE THREE SHOPS

Near the Place Maubert, at the spot where each morning early I wait for the bus, three shops stand side by side: Jewels, Coal and Firewood, Butcher. Observing them in turn, I notice how differently, it seems to me, metal, precious stones, coal, wood chunks, slices of raw meat behave.

We won't linger too long over the metals, which are only the result of man's exploitative or divisive influence on muds or on certain conglomerate rocks that by themselves had no such intentions, nor the precious stones, whose rarity correctly suggests that one give to them only a few exquisite words during a discourse on nature so equitably arranged.

As for the raw meat, a certain shiver as I look, a kind of horror or empathy obliges me to the greatest discretion. Moreover, when freshly sliced, a veil of steam or smoke, sui generis, screens them from the very eyes that would want to reveal certain, one might properly say, cynical thoughts. I will have said all I can say when I have drawn attention for one minute to something *panting* in their appearance.

The contemplation of firewood and coal, however, is a source of delights as immediate as they are sober and certain, which I would be pleased to share. Without doubt, that would require several pages, when in fact I have here only one half of one. That is why I set a limit and propose to you the following subject for your meditations: I. TIME THAT IS OCCUPIED WITH RADIUSES OF A CIRCLE ALWAYS REVENGES ITSELF, BY DEATH. 2. BECAUSE IT IS BROWN, AND BROWN IS MIDWAY BETWEEN GREEN AND BLACK ON THE ROAD TO CARBON, THE WOOD'S DESTINY INVOLVES—THOUGH IN A SMALL DEGREE—A SERIES OF EXPLOITS; THAT IS TO SAY, ERROR ITSELF, MISTAKES, AND EVERY POSSIBLE MISUNDERSTANDING.

THE DELIGHTS OF THE DOOR

Kings don't touch doors.

They don't know this joy: to push affectionately or fiercely before us one of those huge panels we know so well, then to turn back in order to replace it—holding a door in our arms.

The pleasure of grabbing one of those tall barriers to a room abdominally, by its porcelain knot; of this swift fighting, body-to-body, when, the forward motion for an instant halted, the eye opens and the whole body adjusts to its new surroundings.

But the body still keeps one friendly hand on the door, holding it open, then decisively pushes the door away, closing itself in—which the click of the powerful but well-oiled spring pleasantly confirms.

THE *ASSIETTE* (THE PLATE)

During our consecration here, let's be careful not to make this thing that we use every day too pearly. No poetic leap, no matter how brilliant, can speak in a sufficiently flat way about the lowly interval that porcelain occupies between pure spirit and appetite.

Not without some humor, alas (it fits its animal better), the name for its lovely matter was taken from a mollusc shell. And we, a gypsy species, are not to take a seat there. Its substance has been named porcelain, from the Latin — by analogy — *porcellana,* sow vulva. . . . Is that good enough for your appetite?

But all beauty, which suddenly rises from the restlessness of the waves, has its true place on a seashell. . . . Is that too much for pure spirit?

And the *assiette,* whatever you say, rose in a similar way from the sea, and what's more was multiplied instantly by that free-spirited juggler in the wings who takes the place sometimes of the melancholic old man who tosses us with poor grace one sun per day.

That is why you see the *assiette* here in its numerous incarnations, still vibrating as a skipped stone settles at last on the sacred surface of the tablecloth.

Here you have all that one can say about an object which contributes more for living than it offers for reflection.

THE CANDLE

Night at times revives a curious plant whose light makes powerfully furnished rooms fall apart into clumps of shadow.

Its gold leaf stands unmoved, attached to the hollow of a small column of alabaster by a pure black leafstalk.

The seedy moths attack it rather than attacking the too-high moon that turns the woods to mist. But scorched in an instant or overstrained in the skirmish, they all tremble on the brink of a mania close to stupor.

The candle, meanwhile, by the way its rays flicker on the book as it suddenly discharges its original gases urges the reader on—then bends over onto its plate and drowns in what has always fed it.

BLACKBERRIES

On the typographical bushes that the poem forms along a road that leads neither out of the world of objects nor toward the spirit, certain fruits are composed of a gathering of spheres, filled with a drop of ink.

*   *   *

Blacks, pinks, and khakis all together, they present us with the spectacle of family members of distinct ages more than any strong desire to pick them.

I think the seeds are disproportionately big in comparison with the surrounding flesh; that's why the birds are not so interested. So little after all remains with them once the fruits have traveled through them from the beak to the anus.

*   *   *

But the poet on his professional walk learns something; he takes from the blackberries food for thought: "This is how," he says to himself, "the patient efforts of a flower—a delicate one—succeed, and generously, even though defended by a grim entanglement of brambles. Without many other virtues, they are ripe—yes, they are—they are finished blackberries, in the same way as this poem is now finished."

RAIN

The rain falling in the courtyard where I watch adopts three manners, each distinct. Toward the center it is a delicate netting (or net) often with holes, a determined fall, though somewhat lethargic, the drops light enough, an eternal drizzle with no animal vigor, an obsessed particle of the pure meteor. Near the courtyard walls to the right and left, heavier drops are falling, energetically, less absorbed in the mass. A few seem big as a grain of wheat, others big as a pea, still others big as marbles. Flowing on the cornices and the stone sills, the rain moves horizontally, though underneath these same blocky barriers, raindrops hang upside down shaped like bellied lozenges. Along the plain made by a tiny zinc roof which my position overhangs, the rain makes a frail counterpane, given a silky texture by complicated streams that flow over the faintly visible undulations and humps of the roofing. The flow moves through a raingutter nearby with the difficulty of an insubstantial creek with no slope, then all at once it drops off in a ropelike thread utterly vertical, it has a thick enough weave, drops down to the pavement blocks, where it flies apart; and the fragments leap up, and are the tips of luminous laces.

Each of these presences has its own manner, and each has its own particular sound. The rain, taken all together, runs like some complicated invention, fiercely, unpredictable and precise, a clockwork of which the moving agent is the weight associated with a given mass of water vapor in the process of precipitation.

The bell sounds as the water-threads hit the stones, the gluppy sounds of the rainspouts, the light blows on the gong become complicated and resonate all together in a concerto never boring, never without true feeling.

When the stored energy in the spring is gone, certain wheels keep on running for a while anyway, more and more lethargically, then the whole thing comes to a stop. If the sun should reappear, the entire edifice vanishes, the light-filled device goes into thin air: well, it rained.

PABLO NERUDA

SOME POETS DESCRIBE the light of the sun shining at the center of all things. Neruda instead describes the dense planets. As we read his poems, we suddenly see going around us in circles, like herds of mad buffalo or distracted horses, all sorts of created things: balconies, glacial rocks, lost address books, olive oil, pipe organs, dining room tables, notary publics, pumas, the shoes of the dead. His book *Residencia en la Tierra* (*Living on Earth*—the Spanish title suggests being at home on the earth) contains an astounding variety of earthly things, each with its own private life. The fifty-six poems in *Residencia* *I* and *II* were written over a period of ten years—roughly from the time Neruda was twenty-one until he was thirty-one—and they are the greatest surrealist poems yet written in a Western language.

Neruda has a gift for breathing in the sorrow that seems to surround all animals and beings. Many surrealist poets are able to throw themselves for minutes backwards into "the unconscious," but Neruda, like a deep-sea crab, all claws and shell, is able to breathe in the heavy substances that lie beneath the daylight consciousness. He stays on the bottom for hours, and moves around calmly and without hysteria.

There are sulphur-colored birds, and hideous intestines
hanging over the doors of houses that I hate,
and there are false teeth forgotten in a coffeepot,
there are mirrors
that ought to have wept from shame and terror,
there are umbrellas everywhere, and venoms, and umbilical cords.

Next he embarked on a long poem, a geological, biological, and political history of South America. He called it *Canto General,* or a poem about everything. James Wright translated some of these poems marvelously:

It was the twilight of the iguana.
From the rainbow-arch of the battlements,
his long tongue like a lance
sank down in the green leaves,
and a swarm of ants, monks with feet chanting,
crawled off into the jungle,
the guanaco, thin as oxygen
in the wide peaks of cloud,
went along, wearing his shoes of gold,
while the llama opened his honest eyes
on the breakable neatness
of a world full of dew.

Canto General is a massive tome, inspired by Whitman, but it includes coal miners, strikes, corrupt conquistadors, people poisoned by sodium nitrate as well. By now, he was a senator in Chile, under a dictator supported by the United States. Neruda said, "I held my hands up and showed them to the generals / and said: 'I am not a part of this crime.'" The government then sent police to arrest him; after a long trip on horseback over mountains, hiding out every night, he finally got to Mexico. He went to France. The first edition of *Canto General* was published in 1950.

During the middle 1950s, he began publishing an entirely new sort of poem, *Odas Elementales,* odes to simple things, love poems to the things of the world, such as salt, wristwatches, a rabbit killed on the road, a watermelon. I've included here his spirited "Ode to My Socks."

He now had a house on the Chilean shore at Isla Negra, which he filled with hundreds of wooden objects, wooden horses and ships' figureheads. In 1966, he gave a reading at the Poetry Center in New York. It began with a poem of Whitman's. He said, "I don't know how many copies of Whitman I've bought in my life." A few years later, he passed through New York again and spoke to a classroom at Columbia. He was now the ambassador to France. He knew the United States government wanted Allende killed. He said to the audience, "I am on my way to Paris to arrange a loan from the World Bank for Chile. I don't think we'll get it. You can bring us down if you want to, and I think you probably will. But please remember the poem by your great poet Coleridge. If you bring us down, we'll be an albatross around your neck."

PABLO NERUDA was born on July 12, 1904, in a small frontier town in southern Chile, the son of a railroad worker. The father was killed in a fall from his train while Neruda was still a boy. Pablo's given name was Neftali Reyes Basoalto, and his pseudonym was taken very young out of admiration for a nineteenth-century Czech writer.

The governments of South America have a tradition of encouraging young poets by offering them consular posts. When Neruda was twenty-three, he was recognized in this way, and the Chilean government gave him a post in the consular service in the Far East. During the next five years, he lived in turn in Burma, Siam, China, Japan, and India.

Neruda came back to South America in 1932 when he was twenty-eight years old. For a while he was consul in Buenos Aires; he met Lorca there, when Lorca came to Argentina on a lecture tour. *Residencia I* was published in 1933. In 1934, he was assigned to the consulate in Spain.

On July 19, 1936, Franco invaded from North Africa. Neruda, overstepping his power a bit, declared Chile on the side of the Spanish Republic. After being retired as consul, he went to Paris, where he raised money for Spanish refugees, helped by Breton and other French poets, and by Vallejo.

In 1944, the workers from Antofagasta, the nitrate mining section of Chile, asked Neruda to run for senator from their district. He did, and was elected, but later barely escaped with his life.

Pinochet, with the help of the American government, succeeded in bringing Allende down. At that time, Neruda was in a hospital, being treated for cancer; the night Pinochet took over, the Chilean doctors were afraid to continue treatment because of Neruda's sentiments, and he died. His wife, Mathilde, has written of that night. Once he was dead, Pinochet's soldiers and supporters ransacked Neruda's Isla Negra house, broke desks and furniture, burned his letters and unpublished poems. So ended this writer's life.

from TWENTY POEMS OF LOVE AND ONE
ODE OF DESPERATION

1

Body of a woman, white hills, white thighs,
when you surrender, you stretch out like the world.
My body, savage and peasant, undermines you
and makes a son leap in the bottom of the earth.

I was lonely as a tunnel. Birds flew from me.
And night invaded me with her powerful army.
Oh the cups of your breasts! Oh your eyes full of absence!
Oh the roses of your mound! Oh your voice slow and sad!

Body of my woman, I will live on through your marvelousness.
My thirst, my desire without end, my wavering road!
Dark river beds down which the eternal thirst is flowing,
and the fatigue is flowing, and the grief without shore.

6

I remember you as you were that ultimate autumn.
You were a gray beret and the whole being at peace.
In your eyes the fires of the evening dusk were battling,
and the leaves were falling in the waters of your soul.

As attached to my arms as a morning glory,
your sad, slow voice was picked up by the leaves.
Bonfire of astonishment in which my thirst was burning.
Soft blue of hyacinth twisting above my soul.

I feel your eyes travel and the autumn is distant:
gray beret, voice of a bird, and heart like a house
toward which my profound desires were emigrating
and my thick kisses were falling like hot coals.

The sky from a ship. The plains from a hill:
your memory is of light, of smoke, of a still pool!
Beyond your eyes the evening dusks were battling.
Dry leaves of autumn were whirling in your soul.

NOTHING BUT DEATH

There are cemeteries that are lonely,
graves full of bones that do not make a sound,
the heart moving through a tunnel,
in it darkness, darkness, darkness,
like a shipwreck we die going into ourselves,
as though we were drowning inside our hearts,
as though we lived falling out of the skin into the soul.

And there are corpses,
feet made of cold and sticky clay,
death is inside the bones,
like a barking where there are no dogs,
coming out from bells somewhere, from graves somewhere,
growing in the damp air like tears or rain.

Sometimes I see alone
coffins under sail,
embarking with the pale dead, with women that have dead hair,
with bakers who are as white as angels,
and pensive young girls married to notary publics,
caskets sailing up the vertical river of the dead,
the river of dark purple,
moving upstream with sails filled out by the sound of death,
filled by the sound of death which is silence.

Death arrives among all that sound
like a shoe with no foot in it, like a suit with no man in it,
comes and knocks, using a ring with no stone in it, with no finger in it,
comes and shouts with no mouth, with no tongue, with no throat.

Nevertheless its steps can be heard
and its clothing makes a hushed sound, like a tree.

I'm not sure, I understand only a little, I can hardly see,
but it seems to me that its singing has the color of damp violets,
of violets that are at home in the earth,
because the face of death is green,
and the look death gives is green,
with the penetrating dampness of a violet leaf
and the somber color of embittered winter.

But death also goes through the world dressed as a broom,
lapping the floor, looking for dead bodies,
death is inside the broom,
the broom is the tongue of death looking for corpses,
it is the needle of death looking for thread.

Death is inside the folding cots:
it spends its life sleeping on the slow mattresses,
in the black blankets, and suddenly breathes out:
it blows out a mournful sound that swells the sheets,
and the beds go sailing toward a port
where death is waiting, dressed like an admiral.

WALKING AROUND

It so happens I am sick of being a man.
And it happens that I walk into tailor shops and movie houses
dried up, waterproof, like a swan made of felt
steering my way in a water of wombs and ashes.

The smell of barbershops makes me break into hoarse sobs.
The only thing I want is to lie still like stones or wool.
The only thing I want is to see no more stores, no gardens,
no more goods, no spectacles, no elevators.

It so happens I am sick of my feet and my nails
and my hair and my shadow.
It so happens I am sick of being a man.

Still it would be marvelous
to terrify a law clerk with a cut lily,
or kill a nun with a blow on the ear.
It would be great
to go through the streets with a green knife,
letting out yells until I died of the cold.

I don't want to go on being a root in the dark,
insecure, stretched out, shivering with sleep,
going on down, into the moist guts of the earth,
taking in and thinking, eating every day.

I don't want so much misery.
I don't want to go on as a root and a tomb,
alone under the ground, a warehouse with corpses,
half frozen, dying of grief.

That's why Monday, when it sees me coming
with my convict face, blazes up like gasoline,
and it howls on its way like a wounded wheel,
and leaves tracks full of warm blood leading toward the night.

And it pushes me into certain corners, into some moist houses,
into hospitals where the bones fly out the window,
into shoe shops that smell like vinegar,
and certain streets hideous as cracks in the skin.

There are sulphur-colored birds, and hideous intestines
hanging over the doors of houses that I hate,
and there are false teeth forgotten in a coffeepot,
there are mirrors
that ought to have wept from shame and terror,
there are umbrellas everywhere, and venoms, and umbilical cords.

I stroll along serenely, with my eyes, my shoes,
my rage, forgetting everything,
I walk by, going through office buildings and orthopedic shops,
and courtyards with washing hanging from the line:
underwear, towels and shirts from which slow
dirty tears are falling.

from LETTER TO MIGUEL OTERO SILVA, IN CARACAS

When I was writing my love poems, which sprouted out from me
on all sides, and I was dying of depression,
nomadic, abandoned, gnawing on the alphabet,
they said to me: "What a great man you are, Theocritus!"
I am not Theocritus: I took life,
and I faced her and kissed her,
and then went through the tunnels of the mines
to see how other men live.
And when I came out, my hands stained with garbage and sadness,
I held my hands up and showed them to the generals,
and said: "I am not a part of this crime."
They started to cough, showed disgust, left off saying hello,
gave up calling me Theocritus, and ended by insulting me
and assigning the entire police force to arrest me
because I didn't continue to be occupied exclusively with metaphysical
    subjects.
But I had brought joy over to my side.

From then on I started getting up to read the letters
the seabirds bring from so far away,
letters that arrive moist, messages I translate
phrase by phrase, slowly and confidently: I am punctilious
as an engineer in this strange duty.
All at once I go to the window. It is a square
of pure light, there is a clear horizon
of grasses and crags, and I go on working here
among the things I love: waves, rocks, wasps,
with an oceanic and drunken happiness.
But no one likes our being happy, and they cast you

in a genial role: "Now don't exaggerate, don't worry,"
and they wanted to lock me in a cricket cage, where there would be
    tears,
and I would drown, and they could deliver elegies over my grave. . . .

That is why you write your songs, so that someday the disgraced and
    wounded America
can let its butterflies tremble and collect its emeralds
without the terrifying blood of beatings, coagulated
on the hands of the executioners and the businessmen.
I guessed how full of joy you would be, by the Orinoco, singing
probably, or perhaps buying wine for your house,
taking your part in the fight and the exaltation,
with broad shoulders, like the poets of our age—
with light clothes and walking shoes.
Ever since that time, I have been thinking of writing to you,
and when Guillén arrived, running over with stories of you,
which were coming loose everywhere out of his clothes
—they poured out under the chestnuts of my house—
I said to myself: "Now!" and even then I didn't start a letter to you.
But today has been too much for me: not only one seabird,
but thousands have gone past my window,
and I have picked up the letters no one reads, letters they take along
to all the shores of the world until they lose them.
Then in each of those letters I read words of yours,
and they resembled the words I write, and dream of, and put in
    poems,
and so I decided to send this letter to you, which I end here,
so I can watch through the window the world that is ours.

THE UNITED FRUIT CO.

When the trumpet sounded, it was
all prepared on the earth,
and Jehovah parceled out the earth
to Coca-Cola, Inc., Anaconda,
Ford Motors, and other entities:
The Fruit Company, Inc.
reserved for itself the most succulent,
the central coast of my own land,
the delicate waist of America.
It rechristened its territories
as the "Banana Republics"
and over the sleeping dead,
over the restless heroes
who brought about the greatness,
the liberty and the flags,
it established the comic opera:
abolished the independencies,
presented crowns of Caesar,
unsheathed envy, attracted
the dictatorship of the flies,
Trujillo flies, Tacho flies,
Carias flies, Martinez flies,
Ubico flies, damp flies
of modest blood and marmalade,
drunken flies who zoom
over the ordinary graves,
circus flies, wise flies
well trained in tyranny.
Among the bloodthirsty flies
the Fruit Company lands its ships,

taking off the coffee and the fruit;
the treasure of our submerged
territories flow as though
on plates into the ships.

Meanwhile Indians are falling
into the sugared chasms
of the harbors, wrapped
for burial in the mist of the dawn:
a body rolls, a thing
that has no name, a fallen cipher,
a cluster of dead fruit
thrown down on the dump.

MELANCHOLY INSIDE FAMILIES

I keep a blue bottle.
Inside it an ear and a portrait.
When the night dominates
the feathers of the owl,
when the hoarse cherry tree
rips out its lips and makes menacing gestures
with rinds which the ocean wind often perforates —
then I know that there are immense expanses hidden from us,
quartz in slugs,
ooze,
blue waters for a battle,
much silence, many ore-veins
of withdrawals and camphor,
fallen things, medallions, kindnesses,
parachutes, kisses.

It is only the passage from one day to another,
a single bottle moving over the seas,
and a dining room where roses arrive,
a dining room deserted
as a fish bone; I am speaking of
a smashed cup, a curtain, at the end
of a deserted room through which a river passes
dragging along the stones. It is a house
set on the foundations of the rain,
a house of two floors with the required number of windows,
and climbing vines faithful in every particular.

I walk through afternoons, I arrive
full of mud and death,

dragging along the earth and its roots,
and its indistinct stomach in which corpses
are sleeping with wheat,
metals, and pushed-over elephants.

But above all there is a terrifying,
a terrifying deserted dining room,
with its broken olive oil cruets,
and vinegar running under its chairs,
one ray of moonlight tied down,
something dark, and I look
for a companion inside myself:
perhaps it is a grocery store surrounded by the sea
and torn clothing from which sea water is dripping.

It is only a deserted dining room,
and around it there are expanses,
sunken factories, pieces of timber
which I alone know,
because I am sad, and because I travel,
and I know the earth, and I am sad.

Translated by Robert Bly and James Wright

YOUTH

An odor like an acid sword made
of plum branches along the road,
the kisses like sugar in the teeth,
the drops of life slipping on the fingertips,
the sweet sexual fruit,
the yards, the haystacks, the inviting
rooms hidden in the deep houses,
the mattresses sleeping in the past, the savage green valley
seen from above, from the hidden window:
adolescence all sputtering and burning
like a lamp turned over in the rain.

ENIGMAS

You've asked me what the lobster is weaving there with his golden
    feet?
I reply, the ocean knows this.
You say, what is the ascidia waiting for in its transparent bell? What is
    it waiting for?
I tell you it is waiting for time, like you.
You ask me whom the Macrocystis algae hugs in its arms?
Study, study it, at a certain hour, in a certain sea I know.
You question me about the wicked tusk of the narwhal, and I reply by
    describing
how the sea unicorn with a harpoon in it dies.
You inquire about the kingfisher's feathers,
which tremble in the pure strings of the southern tides?
Or you've found in the cards a new question touching on the crystal
    architecture
of the sea anemone, and you'll deal that to me now?
You want to understand the electric nature of the ocean spines?
The armored stalactite that breaks as it walks?
The hook of the angler fish, the music stretched out
in the deep places like a thread in the water?

I want to tell you the ocean knows this, that life in its jewel boxes
is endless as the sand, impossible to count, pure,
and among the blood-colored grapes time has made the petal
hard and shiny, made the jellyfish full of light
and untied its knot, letting its musical threads fall
from a horn of plenty made of infinite mother-of-pearl.
I am nothing but the empty net which has gone on ahead
of human eyes, dead in those darknesses,

of fingers accustomed to the triangle, longitudes
on the timid globe of an orange.

I walked around as you do, investigating
the endless star,
and in my net, during the night, I woke up naked,
the only thing caught, a fish trapped inside the wind.

ODE TO MY SOCKS

Maru Mori brought me
a pair
of socks
which she knitted herself
with her sheepherder's hands,
two socks as soft
as rabbits.
I slipped my feet
into them
as though into
two
cases
knitted
with threads of
twilight
and goatskin.
Violent socks,
my feet were
two fish made
of wool,
two long sharks
sea-blue, shot
through
by one golden thread,
two immense blackbirds,
two cannons:
my feet
were honored
in this way
by

these
heavenly
socks.
They were
so handsome
for the first time
my feet seemed to me
unacceptable,
like two decrepit
firemen, firemen
unworthy
of that woven
fire,
of those glowing
socks.

Nevertheless
I resisted
the sharp temptation
to save them somewhere,
as schoolboys
keep
fireflies,
as learned men
collect
sacred texts,
I resisted
the mad impulse
to put them
into a golden
cage
and each day give them
birdseed

and pieces of pink melon.
Like explorers
in the jungle who hand
over the very rare
green deer
to the spit
and eat it
with remorse,
I stretched out
my feet
and pulled on
the magnificent
socks
and then my shoes.
The moral
of my ode is this:
beauty is twice
beauty
and what is good is doubly
good
when it is a matter of two socks
made of wool
in winter.

ODE TO SALT

I saw the salt
in this shaker
in the salt flats.
I know
you
will never believe me,
but
it sings,
the salt sings, the hide
of the salt plains,
it sings
through a mouth smothered
by earth.
I shuddered in those deep
solitudes
when I heard
the voice
of
the salt
in the desert.
Near Antofagasta
the entire
salt plain
speaks:
it is a
broken
voice,
a song full
of grief.

Then in its own mines
rock salt, a mountain
of buried light,
a cathedral through which light passes,
crystal of the sea, abandoned
by the waves.

And then on every table
on this earth,
salt,
your nimble
body
pouring out
the vigorous light
over
our foods.
Preserver
of the stores
of the ancient ships,
you were
an explorer
in the ocean,
substance
going first
over the unknown, barely open
routes of the sea foam.
Dust of the sea, the tongue
receives a kiss
of the night sea from you:
taste recognizes
the ocean in each salted morsel,
and therefore the smallest,

the tiniest
wave of the shaker
brings home to us
not only your domestic whiteness
but the inward flavor of the infinite.

GEORG TRAKL

IN A TYPICAL Trakl poem, images follow one another in a way that is somehow stately. The rhythm is slow and heavy, like the mood of someone in a dream. Wings of dragonflies, toads, the gravestones of cemeteries, leaves, and war helmets give off strange colors, brilliant and somber colors. Everywhere there is the suggestion of a dark silence:

> The yellow flowers
> Bend without words over the blue pond

The silence is that of things that could speak, but choose not to. As Trakl grew older, more silent creatures agreed to appear in his poems—first it was only wild ducks and dragonflies, but then oak trees, deer, decaying wallpaper, herds of sheep, ponds, and finally steel helmets, armies, wounded men, battlefield nurses, and the blood that had run from the wounds that day.

> Yet a red cloud, in which a furious god,
> The spilled blood itself, has its home, silently
> Gathers, a moonlike coolness in the willow bottoms.

Martin Seymour-Smith has noted that Trakl is not only the visionary poet but the alienated artist as well. His own family equated "poetry" with "failure," and yet his gloom "arose from a consciousness of joy" rather than from decadence. Martin Heidegger showed in his essay on Trakl that "green" is the green both of spring and of decay.

Trakl was influenced by Rimbaud and by Nietzsche, but more deeply by Hölderlin, who was opposed to orthodox religion but was profoundly religious. Austrian culture was in decay in Trakl's time, but he retained great integrity in the midst of that decay. He has many images of a decline going steeply into death or sleep.

Rilke said of him: "Trakl's poetry is to me an object of sublime existence. . . . It occurs to me that his whole work has a parallel in the aspiration of a Li Po: in both, falling is the pretext for the most continuous ascension."

GEORG TRAKL was born in Salzburg in 1887, the son of an iron-monger. The family was partially Czech, but spoke German. While still at school, he began to inhale chloroform and drank heavily. He took a degree in pharmacology in Vienna, and entered military service for a year. He then returned to Salzburg. His sister Margareta, who appears often in his poems, was a concert pianist; she committed suicide. The theme of incest often appears in his poems.

Trakl had a deep commitment to the life of the artist and the work of writing poetry. Some of his letters about that commitment influenced Rilke. Rilke, for his part, never touched drugs, but Trakl could not go on living without them. Ludwig Wittgenstein knew that Trakl was a genius, and he set aside money for Trakl through a patron, Ludwig von Ficker, who published Trakl's poetry in the magazine *Der Brenner*. Only one book of Trakl's poems appeared in his lifetime, a selection made by Franz Werfel, published in 1913. In August of 1914, he was called up as a lieutenant in the Austrian medical corps. He served in the field near Galizia.

After the battle of Grodek, ninety badly wounded men were left in a barn for him to care for. He had no supplies and was not a doctor. That night he attempted to kill himself, but was prevented by friends. The last poems in this selection were written during this time, and the sense of his own approaching death is clear, and set down with astonishing courage. His poem called "Grodek," which is thought to be his last work, is a ferocious poem. It is constructed with great care. A short passage suggesting the whole of German Romantic poetry of the nineteenth century appears, and is followed instantly by a passage evoking the mechanical violence of the German twentieth century. This alternation, so strong that it can even be felt slightly in the translation, gives the poem great strength and fiber.

> At evening the woods of autumn are full of the sound
> Of the weapons of death, golden fields
> And blue lakes, over which the darkening sun
> Rolls down.

After the crisis at Grodek, Trakl went on serving in his post for several months, meanwhile using the drugs obtained from his pharmacy supplies. He was transferred to the hospital at Kraków and assigned, to his surprise, not as a corpsman, but as a patient. He developed a delusion that he would be executed as a deserter. No one was near to help, and he died in November 1914 of an overdose of cocaine, probably unintentionally.

THE SUN

Each day the gold sun comes over the hill.
The woods are beautiful, also the dark animals,
Also man; hunter or farmer.

The fish rises with a red body in the green pond.
Under the arch of heaven
The fisherman travels smoothly in his blue skiff.

The grain, the cluster of grapes, ripen slowly.
When the still day comes to an end,
Both evil and good have been prepared.

When the night has come,
Easily the pilgrim lifts his heavy eyelids;
The sun breaks from gloomy ravines.

SUMMER

At evening the complaint of the cuckoo
Grows still in the wood.
The grain bends its head deeper,
The red poppy.

Darkening thunder drives
Over the hill.
The old song of the cricket
Dies in the field.

The leaves of the chestnut tree
Stir no more.
Your clothes rustle
On the winding stair.

The candle gleams silently
In the dark room;
A silver hand
Puts the light out;

Windless, starless night.

ON THE MARSHY PASTURES

A man who walks in the black wind; the dry reeds rustle quietly
Through the silence of the marshy pastures. In the gray skies
A migration of wild birds moves in ranks
Catty-corner over dark waters.

Insurgence. In the collapsing houses
Decay is fluttering out with black wings;
Crippled-up birches breathe heavily in the wind.

Evening in empty roadhouses. The longing for home settles about
The delicate despair of the grazing flocks,
Vision of the night: toads plunge from silver waters.

SONG OF THE WESTERN COUNTRIES

Oh the nighttime beating of the soul's wings:
Herders of sheep once, we walked along the forests that were
    growing dark,
And the red deer, the green flower and the speaking river followed us
In humility. Oh the old old note of the cricket,
Blood blooming on the altarstone,
And the cry of the lonely bird over the green silence of the pool.

And you Crusades, and glowing punishment
Of the flesh, purple fruits that fell to earth
In the garden at dusk, where young and holy men walked,
Enlisted men of war now, waking up out of wounds and
    dreams about stars.
Oh the soft cornflowers of the night.

And you long ages of tranquillity and golden harvests,
When as peaceful monks we pressed out the purple grapes;
And around us the hill and forest shone strangely.
The hunts for wild beasts, the castles, and at night, the rest,
When a man in his room sat thinking justice,
And in noiseless prayer fought for the living head of God.

And this bitter hour of defeat,
When we behold a stony face in the black waters.
But radiating light, the lovers lift their silver eyelids:
They are one body. Incense streams from rose-colored pillows
And the sweet song of those risen from the dead.

IN HELLBRUNN

Once more following the blue grief of the evening
Down the hill, to the springtime fishpond—
As if the shadows of those dead for a long time were hovering above,
The shadows of church dignitaries, of noble ladies—
Their flowers bloom so soon, the earnest violets
In the earth at evening, and the clear water washes
From the blue spring. The oaks turn green
In such a ghostly way over the forgotten footsteps of the dead,
The golden clouds over the fishpond.

BIRTH

These mountains: blackness, silence, and snow.
The red hunter climbs down from the forest;
Oh the mossy gaze of the wild thing.

The peace of the mother: under black firs
The sleeping hands open by themselves
When the cold moon seems ready to fall.

The birth of man. Each night
Blue water washes over the rockbase of the cliff;
The fallen angel stares at his reflection with sighs,

Something pale wakes up in a suffocating room.
The eyes
Of the stony old woman shine, two moons.

The cry of the woman in labor. The night troubles
The boy's sleep with black wings,
With snow, which falls with ease out of the purple clouds.

THE HEART

The wild heart grew white in the forest;
Dark anxiety
Of death, as when the gold
Died in the gray cloud.
An evening in November.
A crowd of needy women stood at the bare gate
Of the slaughterhouse;
Rotten meat and guts fell
Into every basket;
Horrible food.

The blue dove of the evening
Brought no forgiveness.
The dark cry of trumpets
Traveled in the golden branches
Of the soaked elms,
A frayed flag
Smoking with blood,
To which a man listens
In wild despair.
All your days of nobility, buried
In that red evening!

Out of the dark entrance hall
The golden shape
Of the young girl steps
Surrounded by the pale moon,
The prince's court of autumn,
Black fir trees broken
In the night's storm,
The steep fortress.
O heart
Glittering above in the snowy cold.

DESCENT AND DEFEAT
To Karl Borromäus Heinrich

Over the white fishpond
The wild birds have blown away.
An icy wind drifts from our stars at evening.

Over our graves
The broken forehead of the night is bending.
Under the oaks we veer in a silver skiff.

The white walls of the city are always giving off sound.
Under arching thorns
O my brother blind minute hands we are climbing toward midnight.

THE MOOD OF DEPRESSION

You dark mouth inside me,
You are strong, shape
Composed of autumn cloud,
And golden evening stillness;
In the shadows thrown
By the broken pine trees
A mountain stream turns dark in the green light;
A little town
That piously dies away into brown pictures.

Now the black horses rear
In the foggy pasture.
I think of soldiers!
Down the hill, where the dying sun lumbers,
The laughing blood plunges,
Speechless
Under the oak trees! Oh the hopeless depression
Of an army; a blazing steel helmet
Fell with a clatter from purpled foreheads.

The autumn night comes down so coolly.
With her white habit glittering like the stars
Over the broken human bodies
The convent nurse is silent.

THE EVENING

With the ghostly shapes of dead heroes
Moon, you fill
The growing silence of the forest,
Sickle moon —
With the gentle embraces
Of lovers,
And with ghosts of famous ages
All around the crumbling rocks;
The moon shines with such blue light
Upon the city,
Where a decaying generation
Lives, cold and evil —
A dark future prepared
For the pale grandchild.
Your shadows swallowed by the moon
Sighing upward in the empty goblet
Of the mountain lake.

ON THE EASTERN FRONT

The ominous anger of masses of men
Is like the wild organ of the winter storm,
The purple surge of battle,
Leafless stars.

With broken eyebrows and silver arms
The night waves to dying soldiers.
In the shade of the ash tree of autumn
The souls of the slain are sighing.

A thorny desert surrounds the city.
The moon chases the shocked women
From the bleeding stairways.
Wild wolves have broken through the door.

MOURNING

The dark eagles, sleep and death,
Rustle all night around my head:
The golden statue of man
Is swallowed by the icy comber
Of eternity. On the frightening reef
The purple remains go to pieces,
And the dark voice mourns
Over the sea.
Sister in my wild despair
Look, a precarious skiff is sinking
Under the stars,
The face of night whose voice is fading.

GRODEK

At evening the woods of autumn are full of the sound
Of the weapons of death, golden fields
And blue lakes, over which the darkening sun
Rolls down; night gathers in
Dying recruits, the animal cries
Of their burst mouths.
Yet a red cloud, in which a furious god,
The spilled blood itself, has its home, silently
Gathers, a moonlike coolness in the willow bottoms;
All the roads spread out into the black mold.
Under the gold branches of the night and stars
The sister's shadow falters through the diminishing grove,
To greet the ghosts of the heroes, bleeding heads;
And from the reeds the sound of the dark flutes of autumn rises.
O prouder grief! you bronze altars,
The hot flame of the spirit is fed today by a more monstrous pain,
The unborn grandchildren.

RAINER MARIA RILKE

RILKE HAS FOR hundreds of readers been their first introduction to poetry that goes steeply and unapologetically up with the spirit. One could say that when a young man or woman encounters him, he will slip his hand under the elbow and guide the person on to some small house that stands nearby, perhaps a hut where the railway switchman lives. Once inside, the young person notices that the ceiling is higher than one would have thought. In fact, the hut is a cathedral, with immensely high vaults, like Chartres, with deep shadows. Meanwhile, Rilke pretends that nothing unusual has happened.

Rilke, when in Paris, often lived in a rented room, sometimes one where a lonely violinist who is staying next door plays all night. Something about that lonely music coming through the wall is right for Rilke's life. He writes magnificently about nature, especially the fall, and he's a great love poet; but in the end he loves great works of art more than nature or human life. Looking at a statue of Buddha he notices that

> [S]omething has already started to live
> in you that will live longer than the sun.

He is an acute observer of human beings; for example, the way a blind woman walks across a room. He does that well, but when he is really concentrated, he describes — as no one else can — a stone statue of Apollo. If a work of art is true, he says,

There is no place at all
that isn't looking at you. You'll have to change your life.

Poets like to write about what the world is like after a hurricane, or after a rainstorm, but Rilke likes to write about what the world is like after a great work of art has been created. That work of art changes the normal world. He wants you to give up all the miscellaneous collection of memories that the poetry workshops encourage, and become serious—move toward great art. His emphasis on great art offends many critics so much, they don't even mention it. What's more, Rilke doesn't say art is born out of life; he says art gives birth to art, and you need to study great artists if you want to write. What is music? Great music doesn't depend on human life, but on music itself. Music is "a statue breathing." Music doesn't give "impressions" of a landscape. It is a "countryside we can hear. . . . The deepest thing in us, that forces its way out . . . as the other side of the air."

We know that in ancient Greece, when a road forked, someone often built a temple there, so that the traveler could decide which way to go. Today, we are in trouble, Rilke says, because where two roads fork "no one has built Apollo's temple." Poetry doesn't mean talking well, but being truly alive. Poetry is "a god breathing." This is highly offensive to many people, and they often refuse to read him. He doesn't care.

Those who attack Rilke for being too "aesthetic" or spiritual miss the point. Neruda and he were opposites, and Neruda once wrote a poem attacking Rilke for being too "celestial." But they are both great artists and both are warriors. Rilke takes "the way less traveled." He urges you to change your life in such a way that you can actually take in the Buddhist art, the art of Greeks, "the deepest thing in us."

RAINER MARIA RILKE was born on December 4, 1875, in Prague, and baptized René Karl Wilhelm Johann Josef Maria Rilke. The many names became suggestive of the various personalities that he carried all his life. His father, after a brief career as a gunner, became a civil servant in the North Bohemian Railway. His mother, who had once lived in a large mansion which belonged to an old Prague family, didn't accept reality well. She refused to acknowledge that Rainer was a boy; she actually put him in dresses and sent him out in the hall to knock on the door. He had to give a girl's name to get in. He describes his mother in *"Aus Einer Kindheit."* In his twenties, he became friends with a group of painters living at Worpswede. He fell in love with one of them, and married another, Clara Westhoff. The couple, who had a daughter named Ruth, did not live together after 1902, though they wrote elaborate letters to each other year after year, often astonishing ones.

He accepted an offer from Rodin in 1906 to be his secretary, and he moved to Meudon near Paris. His close connection to Rodin lasted two years. He remarked that Rodin's influence made him see more. Rodin actually told him if he couldn't write he should go to the zoo and look at a panther. Out of this exercise came *New Poems,* published in 1908, great poems on the movement of a swan in water, on the way a panther walks in a cage, and the like. In 1915, the German government drafted him into the army, and he worked during 1916 as an archivist in Vienna. A long fallow period followed. All at once, in a huge burst of energy, he wrote both the *Duino Elegies* and the *Sonnets to Orpheus.* In his view of his own life, he had now done his work. As it turned out, he had only three more years to live. During this time he stayed in a small tower in Switzerland where he continued to write astonishing poems. His leukemia was not diagnosed correctly for two years, and he died at Muzot in 1926 at the age of fifty-one.

THE MAN WATCHING

I can tell by the way the trees beat, after
so many dull days, on my worried windowpanes
that a storm is coming,
and I hear the far-off fields saying things
I can't bear without a friend,
I can't love without a sister.

The storm, the shifter of shapes, drives on
across the woods and across time,
and the world looks as if it had no age:
the landscape, like a line in the psalm book,
is seriousness and weight and eternity.

What we choose to fight is so tiny!
What fights with us is so great!
If only we would let ourselves be dominated
as things do by some immense storm,
we would become strong too, and not need names.

When we win it's with small things,
and the triumph itself makes us small.
What is extraordinary and eternal
does not *want* to be bent by us.
I mean the Angel who appeared
to the wrestlers of the Old Testament:
when the wrestlers' sinews
grew long like metal strings,
he felt them under his fingers
like chords of deep music.

Whoever was beaten by this Angel
(who often simply declined the fight)
went away proud and strengthened
and great from that harsh hand,
that kneaded him as if to change his shape.
Winning does not tempt that man.
This is how he grows: by being defeated, decisively,
by constantly greater beings.

I LIVE MY LIFE IN GROWING ORBITS

I live my life in growing orbits
which move out over the things of the world.
Perhaps I can never achieve the last,
but that will be my attempt.

I am circling around God, around the ancient tower,
and I have been circling for a thousand years,
and I still don't know if I am a falcon, or a storm,
or a great song.

SOMETIMES A MAN STANDS UP DURING SUPPER

Sometimes a man stands up during supper
and walks outdoors, and keeps on walking,
because of a church that stands somewhere in the East.

And his children say blessings on him as if he were dead.

And another man, who remains inside his own house,
dies there, inside the dishes and in the glasses,
so that his children have to go far out into the world
toward that same church, which he forgot.

I AM TOO ALONE IN THE WORLD

I am too alone in the world, and not alone enough
to make every minute holy.
I am too tiny in this world, and not tiny enough
just to lie before you like a thing,
shrewd and secretive.
I want my own will, and I want simply to be with my will,
as it goes toward action,
and in the silent, sometimes hardly moving times
when something is coming nearer,
I want to be with those who know secret things
or else alone.
I want to be a mirror for your whole body,
and I never want to be blind, or to be too old
to hold up your heavy and swaying picture.
I want to unfold.
I don't want to stay folded anywhere,
because where I am folded, there I am a lie.
And I want my grasp of things
true before you. I want to describe myself
like a painting that I looked at
closely for a long time,
like a saying that I finally understood,
like the pitcher I use every day,
like the face of my mother,
like a ship
that took me safely
through the wildest storm of all.

SONNETS TO ORPHEUS, VII

To praise is the whole thing! A man who can praise
comes toward us like ore out of the silences
of rock. His heart, that dies, presses out
for others a wine that is fresh forever.

When the god's energy takes hold of him,
his voice never collapses in the dust.
Everything turns to vineyards, everything turns to grapes,
made ready for harvest by his powerful south.

The mold in the catacomb of the king
does not suggest that his praising is lies, nor
the fact that the gods cast shadows.

He is one of the servants who does not go away,
who still holds through the doors
of the tomb trays of shining fruit.

THE SWAN

This clumsy living that moves lumbering
as if in ropes through what is not done
reminds us of the awkward way the swan walks.

And to die, which is a letting go
of the ground we stand on and cling to every day,
is like the swan when he nervously lets himself down

into the water, which receives him gaily
and which flows joyfully under
and after him, wave after wave,
while the swan, unmoving and marvelously calm,
is pleased to be carried, each minute more fully grown,
more like a king, composed, farther and farther on.

ARCHAIC TORSO OF APOLLO

We have no idea what his fantastic head
was like, where the eyeballs were slowly swelling. But
his body now is glowing like a gas lamp,
whose inner eyes, only turned down a little,

hold their flame, shine. If there weren't light, the curve
of the breast wouldn't blind you, and in the swerve
of the thighs a smile wouldn't keep on going
toward the place where the seeds are.

If there weren't light, this stone would look cut off
where it drops clearly from the shoulders,
its skin wouldn't gleam like the fur of a wild animal,

and the body wouldn't send out light from every edge
as a star does . . . for there is no place at all
that isn't looking at you. You'll have to change your life.

DAY IN OCTOBER

Lord, the time has come. The summer was immense.
Lay down your shadow on the sundials,
and on the open places let the winds go free.

Give the tardy fruits the hint to fill;
give them two more Mediterranean days,
drive them on into their greatness, and press
the final sweetness into the heavy wine.

Whoever has no house by now will not build one.
Whoever is alone will be a long time alone,
will stay up, read, write long letters,
and then in the wide avenues drift restlessly
here and there, as the withered leaves blow by.

I FIND YOU

I find you in all these things of the world
that I love calmly, like a brother;
in things no one cares for you brood like a seed;
and to powerful things you give an immense power.

Strength plays such a marvelous game—
it moves through the things of the world like a servant,
groping out in roots, tapering in trunks,
and in the treetops like a rising from the dead.

"WE MUST DIE BECAUSE WE HAVE KNOWN THEM"

from Papyrus Prisse. From the sayings of Ptah-Hotep, 6th Dynasty (2300–1650 BCE)

"We must die because we have known them." Die
of the unbelievable flower of their smile. Die
of their delicate hands. Die of women.

The adolescent boy praises the death-givers,
when they float magnificently through his
heart halls. From his blossoming body
he cries out to them:
impossible to reach. Oh, how strange they are.
They go swiftly over
the peaks of his emotions and pour down
the marvelously altered night into his deserted
arm valley. The wind that rises
in their dawn makes his body leaves rustle. His brooks
glisten away in the sun.

But the grown man
shivers and says nothing. The man
who blundered around all night
on the mountains of his feelings remains
silent.

As the old sailor remains silent,
and the terrors
he's experienced leap about in him as if in rocking cages.

PARIS, JULY 1914

BUDDHA INSIDE THE LIGHT

The core of every core, the kernel of every kernel,
an almond! held in itself, deepening in sweetness:
all of this, everything, right up to the stars,
is the meat around your stone. Accept my bow.

Oh, yes, you feel it, how the weights on you are gone!
Your husk has reached into what has no end,
and that is where the great saps are brewing now.
On the outside a warmth is helping,

for, high, high above, your own suns are growing
immense and they glow as they wheel around.
Yet something has already started to live
in you that will live longer than the sun.

from THE LIFE OF THE VIRGIN MARY

1. The Birth of Mary

Oh what it must have cost the angels
Not to break out singing (as we burst in tears),
For they knew well that this night was the Night
Of the Mother's birth . . . whose son would soon be here.

In their silence the angels pointed out from the air
Where Joachim's farm stood by itself in the field.
They could feel the Great Descending all around
And in their beings, but no descending was allowed.

The farm couple were already half out of it.
A neighbor woman came and talked and knew nothing;
And the old man went out and consciously
Quieted a dark cow. Nothing like this ever.

2. Mary Presented at the Temple

In order to understand how Mary was at that
Moment, you'd have to find some place inside you
Where pillars hold you up, where you can feel
Stairways, where arches give support to
A perilous bridge over some deep space which
Endured in you simply because it was built up
Out of rocks that you couldn't possibly lift
Now out of yourself or you would bring yourself down.
If you're so far along that everything in you is stone,
Great walls, ascending stairs, views, domes—then try
To pull aside with both hands that great hanging cloth
Just in front of your face, a little at least.

The light of glory shines down from the high things
More powerful than your breath or your feelings.
One palace over another palace, from below, from above,
Parapets rise out of deeper parapets
Finally emerging so high up that you, if
You took it in, would be afraid of falling.
Meanwhile, clouds of incense from the burners
Trouble the air around you, but the most distinct things
Aim straight at you with their steady beam.
And when next the clear flames of the burning lamps
Play over the elaborate robes that are approaching
Could you endure this?
But she did come, and lifted her
Eyes and addressed the whole scene.
(A child, a half-grown girl among grown women)
She mounted the stair calmly, knowing who she was,
Toward this great extravagance which shifted to meet her.
Everything that people have built was already
Deeply outweighed by the praise that remained
In her heart. And by the urge
To give herself over to the inner presence:
Her parents' plan was just to bring her there, present her.
The scary man with his chest of jewels
Seemed to receive her. But she went on through,
Small as she was, past every hand
On into her destiny which is now complete,
Higher than the building, heavier than the whole temple.

4. Mary's Visit with Elizabeth
It all went well from the very start,
Although sometimes when climbing she was aware
Of the amazing thing far inside her body.
Then she would stop, and breathe, on the top of a high

Hill in Judea. It wasn't the land around her,
It was her own abundance that surrounded her.
As she walked she felt: No woman will ever
Have any more largeness than I have now.

And she recognized a longing to place her hand
On her cousin's big belly, farther along toward birth.
The two women bent toward each other;
Each touched the other's dress and touched the hair.

Each one, full of her own holy treasure,
Found a safe place at the side of her kin.
Ah, the Savior in Mary was only a blossom
But the joy of it roused the little Baptist
In the womb to hop and leap about.

5. The Suspicions of Joseph

And the Angel spoke, not without carefully hearing
This man who stood there with his fists tightened.
"But isn't it clear from every fold of her dress
That she is as cool as the morning mist?"

The man however looked suspiciously back
And said, "I want to know how this happened."
The Angel spoke louder: "You woodworker,
Don't you see any mark of God at all in this?

"Just because you know how to make planks
Out of tree trunks, are you unable to imagine
One who can bring forth leaves
And pregnant buds out of the same wood?"

He got it. And the instant he lifted
His deeply shocked eyes to the Angel,
The Angel was gone. He took hold of his cap
And pulled it off slowly. And what he sang was a hymn.

12. The Quiet Mary Knew with the Risen Christ

What they felt was this: Isn't it
Fantastically sweet beyond all other mysteries,
And yet immensely earthbound:
That he, slightly pale still from the grave,
Walked light as air toward her,
Risen in every particle of his being.
Oh it was to her first. Far beyond speech
They felt that healing.
Yes, healing was what it was
And there was no need for firm touch.
He laid for a second only
His hand, about to be
Eternal, on her woman's shoulder.
And they began
As quietly as trees in April,
Wholly mingled,
The new season
Of their deepest union.

PALM

Palm of the hand. Sole, that walks now
only on feeling. The hand turns over
and in its mirror
shows heavenly roads, that themselves are
walking.
It has learned to stroll on water
when it dips down,
walks on top of fountains,
causes all roads to fork.
It steps forward into another's hand,
changes its doubles
into a countryside,
travels into them and arrives,
fills them with having arrived.

MUZOT, OCTOBER 1924

ON MUSIC

Music: the breathing of statues. Perhaps:
the silence of paintings. Language where
language ends. Time
that stands head-up in the direction
        of hearts that wear out.

Feeling . . . for whom? Place where feeling is
transformed . . . into what? Into a countryside we can hear.
Music: you stranger. You feeling space, growing
away from us. The deepest thing in us, that,
rising above us, forces its way out . . .
a holy goodbye:
when the innermost point in us stands
outside, as amazing space, as the other
side of the air:
pure,
immense,
not for us to live in now.

MUNICH, JANUARY 1918

A WALK

My eyes already touch the sunny hill,
going far ahead of the road I have begun.
So we are grasped by what we cannot grasp;
it has its inner light, even from a distance —

and changes us, even if we do not reach it,
into something else, which, hardly sensing it, we already are;
a gesture waves us on, answering our own wave . . .
but what we feel is the wind in our faces.

MUZOT, MARCH 1924

JUST AS THE WINGED ENERGY OF DELIGHT

Just as the winged energy of delight
carried you over many chasms early on,
now raise the daringly imagined arch
holding up the astounding bridges.

Miracle doesn't lie only in the amazing
living through and defeat of danger;
miracles become miracles in the clear
achievement that is earned.

To work with things is not hubris
when building the association beyond words;
denser and denser the pattern becomes—
being carried along is not enough.

Take your well-disciplined strengths
and stretch them between two
opposing poles. Because inside human beings
is where God learns.

MUZOT, FEBRUARY 1924

BASHO

FOR THE HAIKU poets, the cry of a mosquito is just as important as a general's hat or a storm. Basho, in his poems, reaches out to a time before birth and after death as well. Observing an autumn evening, he remarks that, "Hades must be a little like this." He often feels Buddha's presence, and the old monks who were masters of meditation. He remarks:

Dried salmon
and Kuya's breakthrough into the spirit—both
belong to the cold time of the year!

A simple walk can be—and he likes it to be—a meditation:

It's fall and a full moon.
I walked around the shore
of the pond all night.

He wrote apparently a thousand haiku. His task was to revive the power of the haiku at a time when the form had become academic and conceptual. He took long walks often in wild weather so he could register every tiny event; but it's always as if some spiritual master were looking over the shoulder of the poem. He is aware of how long the spiritual road is, the Road to the Deep North. Dogen wrote poems but thought of himself more as a teacher of enlightenment than as a poet, but Basho always stayed in nature. Lucien Stryk remarked that he "strove to place his reader within an experience whose unfolding might lead to revelation."

In *Records of a Worn-Out Knapsack*, he said something like this:

> Inside this pitiful body which has one hundred bones and nine holes, there is something called spirit, which is like a flowing curtain easily blown around by wind. It was spirit that got me to writing poetry, at first for amusement, later as a way of life. At times, my spirit has been brought down so low that I almost quit writing, and at other times the spirit became proud and powerful. It's been like that from the start: the spirit never is at peace, always in doubt of the value of what it does. Sometimes it has been attracted to life at court, at another time it's been leaning toward the dangerous life of a scholar. But the spirit would not allow either route; it stuck to haiku. Artists who have achieved greatness—Saigyon in poetry, Sogi in linked verse, Sesshu in painting, Rikyu in tea ceremony—each of them obeys the spirit. They all possess one thing in common. Each remains through the four seasons at one with nature.

Basho warned readers about the animalistic—or "barbarian"—heart and mind. He asked for haiku poets to adopt elegance and "lightness," which results from the well-known quality of "nonattachment":

> Skylark in the waste fields —
> one sweet cry
> of nonattachment.

BASHO was born Matsuo Munefusa in 1644 in a small town named Ueno, some thirty miles southeast of Kyoto. His father died when he was twelve. Basho entered the service of a local feudal lord at that time. When the lord died ten years later, Basho left his hometown and traveled, perhaps to Kyoto, for the first time. He then studied with a well-known priest, and edited a collection of haiku, to which thirty poets contributed poems. In 1680, when he was thirty-six, his students built a hut for him on the Sumita River, near a large banana tree, or *basho*. He took that name for himself. As the hut would burn down, a new one would be built. He lived sparsely, and believed that nature is what is important. When he was about forty, he began a series of wanderings or long walks. Taking only his knapsack and a stick, he would walk for miles and miles, writing haiku on what he saw. He described his first trip in *Travel Diary of Weathered Bones*. He also published accounts of a trip to Kenshin Shrine, and to Sarashao, and another long trip to various places, which resulted in *Records of a Worn-Out Knapsack*. Finally, when he was forty-five, he journeyed north to the provinces of Honshu. From that came *The Narrow Road to the Deep North*, probably his most famous book.

In the five years that he still had left to live, he suffered often from headaches and fevers. He built a hut for the third time, and wrote *Commentaries on an Autumn Night*. He constantly helped others with their haiku, and always complained that he had too much social life and not enough solitude. At one point he closed his gate and refused to see visitors. He took one more walking trip and then died in Osaka when he was fifty years old.

Spider, if you had a voice,
what would you sing,
swaying in the fall wind?

It's fall and dusk.
And no one is walking
along the road.

The temple bell stops—
but the sound keeps coming
out of the flowers.

It's late fall.
I wonder how the man
next door lives.

It's fall and a full moon.
I walked around the shore
of the pond all night.

Dried salmon
and Kuya's breakthrough into the spirit—both
belong to the cold time of the year!

Storm on Mount Asama!
Wind blowing
out of the stones!

Give your longing to wound
and to own more things
away to the willow.

The sea grows rough.
The Milky Way reaches past
the islands of Sado!

How marvelous the man is
who can see a lightning flash
and not think, "Life is short!"

It's spring, all right;
that hill we never named
is hidden in the mist.

The sea grows dark.
The voices of wild ducks
turn white.

It's quiet, all right.
The cries of the cicadas
sink into the rocks.

Octopuses caught in floating pots,
dreams that are not eternal
under the summer moon.

ROLF JACOBSEN

IN SOME WAYS, Rolf Jacobsen was the first "modern" poet in
Norway. He began writing poems in the thirties. By then cars were
becoming common, and their tires were softer than they are now. He
noticed that the *F* of Firestone was pressed into the sand of a forest
road going along between pines.

> [A] car had passed by on the dusty road
> where an ant was out with his pine needle working
> he was wandering around in the huge *F* of Firestone
> that had been pressed into the sandy earth
> for a hundred and twenty kilometers.

We too have been pressed into the sandy earth. We too are wandering
around in the *F* of Firestone.

Even in the thirties, some people in Norway did feel abandoned in
the cities. He mentions a street lamp in the city that holds up its light
umbrella over the paving stones "so that the wicked dark will not
come near." The street lamp speaks:

> It says: We are all far from home.
> There's no hope anymore.

In the old Norway of the deep forests, there was always hope. If
you walked long enough you'd come to a well-built group of farm

buildings, perhaps with a lame old man out in front, chopping wood. He'd invite you in for dinner. But in the city—in Oslo—that did not happen.

> Let the young rain of tears come.
> Let the calm hands of grief come.
> It's not all as evil as you think.

So we have a poet who is sensitive to contemporary loneliness; and yet he is able to produce exquisitely tender riffs almost like Mozart in their elegance. He is a willing participant in the invisible world. He refuses to be a pedestrian; he does not complain; he is not elsewhere. He is willing to go to that bodiless world where the invisibles live above us or below us, unusual for a poet of his generation.

So we have something remarkable in Jacobsen—someone who lives in the same disappointing world in which we all live, and yet is willing to imagine glory: he is willing to praise the beauty of this populated earth. He sees a lot of things wrong with human beings, and yet he is willing to look at people almost without judgment, like a Buddhist:

> Some people
> ascend out of our life, some people
> enter our life,
>   uninvited and sit down . . .
>   some people
> eat asparagus, some people
> are children,
> some people climb up on the roof,
> sit down at table,

lie around in hammocks . . . some people
want to take your hand, some people
die during the night,
some people are other people, some people are you, some people
don't exist,
some people do.

ROLF JACOBSEN was born in Oslo, March 8, 1907. For most of his
life, he lived in Hamar, north and east of Oslo. He worked as an editor
for the local newspaper, many times taking the night shift. In his first
book, *Earth and Iron,* he took on himself the task of writing about
iron, as well as about the old Norwegian poetic subject, the earth itself.
To the astonishment of many readers, a number of the poems were in
free verse, and were not rhymed. He brought trains in, gaslights, tele-
phone poles, telescopes, advertisements for scotch whisky, steam shov-
els, as well as the stave churches and the old forests. He remarked on
interesting developments as well, noticing that the age of the great
symphonies was now over, but the magnificent sound continues to
"pour down like rain" into the farmer's living room, "a sack of noise."
After World War II, he became more skeptical of technology's
promise, and of the consumer society. Altogether he produced twelve
books of poems, and he received the Norwegian Critics' Prize in 1960,
the Aschehoug Prize in 1986, the Bergen Prize in 1968, and the "little
Nobel Prize," the Grand Nordic Prize from the Swedish Academy in
1989. He went on a reading tour of the United States during the
eighties. When his wife, Petra, to whom he had been married for
forty-three years, became ill and died in 1983, he wrote a sequence of
poems for her that was published in his last book, *Night Watch,* in
1985. These poems have been beautifully translated by Roger
Greenwald. Even though Norway is a small country, 15,000 copies of

that book were sold, more than are sold for most poets in the United States.

During the last years of his life, he became friends with Olav H. Hauge. Jacobsen's poems were translated into more than twenty languages. He died when he was eighty-seven years old, in 1994.

COUNTRY ROADS

A pale morning in June, 4 A.M.
the country roads still grayish and moist
tunneling endlessly through pines
a car had passed by on the dusty road
where an ant was out with his pine needle working
he was wandering around in the huge *F* of Firestone
that had been pressed into the sandy earth
for a hundred and twenty kilometers.
Fir needles are heavy.
Time after time he slipped back with his badly
   balanced
   load
and worked it up again
and skidded back again
traveling over the great and luminous Sahara lit by clouds.

MOON AND APPLE

When the apple tree blooms,
the moon comes often like a blossom,
paler than any of them,
shining over the tree.

It is the ghost of the summer,
the white sister of the blossoms who returns
to drop in on us,
and radiate peace with her hands
so that you shouldn't feel too bad when the hard times come.
For the Earth itself is a blossom, she says,
on the star tree,
pale and with luminous
ocean leaves.

THE AGE OF THE GREAT SYMPHONIES

The age of the great symphonies
is over now.

The symphonies rose toward heaven with real magnificence—
sunlit clouds with thunder in
over the brilliant centuries.
Cumulus under blue skies. Coriolanus.

Now they are coming back down again in the form of rain,
a banded, stone-colored rain on all the wavelengths and programs
covering earth like a wet overcoat, a sack of noise.

Now they are coming back down from the sky,
they bounce off the skyscrapers like electric hail
and seep down into farmers' living rooms
and roll over the suburbs and brick-oceans
as immortal sound.
A rain of sound,
"You millions of this earth, embrace,"
so as to deaden screams

every day, every day
on this earth which is thirsty and takes them back into itself again.

SUNFLOWER

What sower walked over earth,
which hands sowed
our inward seeds of fire?
They went out from his fists like rainbow curves
to frozen earth, young loam, hot sand,
they will sleep there
greedily, and drink up our lives
and explode it into pieces
for the sake of a sunflower that you haven't seen
or a thistle head or a chrysanthemum.

Let the young rain of tears come.
Let the calm hands of grief come.
It's not all as evil as you think.

LIGHT POLE

My street lamp is so glacially alone in the night.
The small paving stones lay their heads down all around
where it holds up its lightumbrella over them
so that the wicked dark will not come near.

It says: We are all far from home.
There's no hope anymore.

ROAD'S END

The roads have come to their end now,
they don't go any farther, they turn here,
over on the earth there.
You can't go any farther if you don't want
to go to the moon or the planets. Stop now
in time, and turn to a wasp's nest or a cow track,
a volcano opening or a clatter of stones in the woods—
it's all the same. Something else.

They won't go any farther as I've said
without changing, the engine to horseshoes,
the gear shift to a fir branch
    which you hold loose in your hand
—what the hell is this?

THE OLD WOMEN

The girls whose feet moved so fast, where did they go?
Those with knees like small kisses and sleeping hair?

In the far reaches of time when they've become silent,
old women with narrow hands climb up stairs slowly

with huge keys in their bags and they look around
and chat with small children at cemetery gates.

In that big and bewildering country where winters are so long
and no one understands their expressions anymore.

Bow clearly to them and greet them with respect
because they still carry everything with them, like a fragrance,

a secret bite-mark on the cheek, a nerve deep in
the palm of the hand somewhere betraying who they are.

GUARDIAN ANGEL

I am the bird that flutters against your window in the morning,
and your closest friend, whom you can never know,
blossoms that light up for the blind.

I am the glacier shining over the woods, so pale,
and heavy voices from the cathedral tower.
The thought that suddenly hits you in the middle of the day
and makes you feel so fantastically happy.

I am the one you have loved for many years.
I walk beside you all day and look intently at you
and put my mouth against your heart
though you're not aware of it.

I am your third arm, and your second
shadow, the white one,
whom you cannot accept,
and who can never forget you.

OLD AGE

I put a lot of stock in the old.
They sit looking at us and don't see us,
and have plenty with their own,
like fishermen along big rivers,
motionless as a stone
in the summer night.

I put a lot of stock in fishermen along rivers
and old people and those who appear after a long illness.
They have something in their eyes
that you don't see much anymore
the old, like convalescents
whose feet are not very sturdy under them
and pale foreheads as if after a fever.

The old
who so gradually become themselves once more
and so gradually break up
like smoke, no one notices it, they are gone
into sleep
and light.

MEMORIES OF HORSES

The lines in the hands of old people
gradually curve over and will point soon toward earth.
They take with them their secret language,
cloud-words and wind-letters,
all the signs the heart gathers up in the lean year.

Sorrow bleaches out and turns to face the stars
but memories of horses, women's feet, children
flow from their old people's faces down to the grass kingdom.

In huge trees we can often see
images of the peace in the sides of animals,
and the wind sketches in the grass, if you are happy,
running children and horses.

THE OLD CLOCKS

The old clocks often have encouraging faces.
They are like those farmers in the big woods or in the mountains
Whose whole being contains some calm acceptance
As if they belonged to some other race than ours.
A race that has fought its way through its time down here
And has seen its unhappiness shrink back like grass
During that earlier period when the Earth was earth.

They are guests with us this time and they nod in tune to our distress
Next to our bed with their mild wisdom: it's OK,
Oh yes, oh yes, it's OK, it's OK.

THE SILENCE AFTERWARDS

Try to be done now
with deliberately provocative actions and sales statistics,
brunches and gas ovens,
be done with fashion shows and horoscopes,
military parades, architectural contests,
and the rows of triple traffic lights.
Come through all that and be through
with getting ready for parties and eight possibilities
of winning on the numbers,
cost of living indexes and stock market analyses,
because it is too late,
it is way too late,
get through with and come home
to the silence afterwards
that meets you like warm blood hitting your forehead
and like thunder on the way
and the sound of great clocks striking
that make the eardrums quiver,
because words don't exist any longer,
there are no more words,
from now on all talk will take place
with the voices stones and trees have.

The silence that lives in the grass
on the underside of every blade
and in the blue spaces between the stones.
The silence
that follows shots and birdsong.
The silence

that pulls a blanket over the dead body
and waits in the stairs until everyone is gone.
The silence
that lies like a small bird between your hands,
the only friend you have.

SOME PEOPLE

Some people
ascend out of our life, some people
enter our life,
uninvited and sit down,
some people
calmly walk by, some people
give you a rose,
or buy you a new car,
some people
stand so close to you, some people
you've entirely forgotten,
some people, some people
are actually you,
some people
you've never seen at all, some people
eat asparagus, some people
are children,
some people climb up on the roof,
sit down at table,
lie around in hammocks, take walks with their red
umbrella,
some people look at you,
some people have never noticed you at all, some people
want to take your hand, some people
die during the night,
some people are other people, some people are you, some people
don't exist,
some people do.

GUNNAR EKELÖF

GUNNAR EKELÖF IS not a well-adjusted writer, happy to be living on earth. His work makes people uncomfortable; he tries to make the reader conscious of lies, and of the unstable and shifty nature of human perception. He doesn't particularly bother about how many readers like his poems. When he says something which he knows is too difficult for the reader to understand, he looks back and laughs. Sometimes he veers off mischievously into a side path that is too narrow anyway. His intelligence is awake all through the poem, cutting away nonsense, like a swift knife thin as gold leaf, cutting away soft and pulpy egoism. He cuts away egoism because he knows that if the Westerner can cut down the pride of his well-fed ego, if the self-contentments can be swept away, he stands some chance of experiencing the floating state the Eastern meditators value so much.

> Ask for a filter for all these things that separate us from one another
> a filter for life
> You say you can hardly breathe?
> Well, who do you think *can* breathe?
> For the most part we take it however with equanimity
> A wise man has said:
> "It was so dark I could barely see the stars"
> He just meant that it was night.

He is an oblique, arrogant, nervous, witty poet of the European city, a sort of poet known in all Western countries. Yet early on, he

reached out to two sources which were outside the Scandinavian tra-
dition: to the mystical poetry of Persia and to French poetry, especially
the surrealist poetry of the late twenties.

At the same time, curious images slip into Ekelöf's poems from the
North. These other images have risen from the heathen Swedish
ground, from old Finnish swamps and that part of the Northern
unconscious still obsessed by shamanic hallucinations, changing of
bodies, journeys of souls during trance.

> I heard wild geese over the hospital grounds
> one autumnlike spring morning
> I heard wild geese one morning
> one springautumn morning
> trumpeting—
>
> To the north? To the south?
> To the north! To the north!
> Far from here—
>
> A freshness lives deep in me
> which no one can take from me
> not even I myself—

GUNNAR EKELÖF was born in 1907 in Stockholm to a wealthy
family. His father contracted syphilis and died, after years of insanity,
in 1916. Ekelöf and his mother were not close, and he left home soon
after passing his high school examinations. He studied at the School
of Oriental Studies in London, and read Persian and Sanskrit in
Uppsala. He moved to Paris at the end of the 1920s, and intended to
become a musician. However, it was French painting and poetry,
especially Desnos and Breton, which attracted him. His first book of

poetry, *Late Arrival on Earth,* in 1932, is thought of as the first book of surrealist poetry in Sweden.

He began to admire T. S. Eliot, and translated "East Coker." He thought of poetry as giving off waves of meaning, almost like a radioactive bit of matter; he preferred that to identifiable content. In 1934, he published *Dedication,* which included a quotation from Rimbaud, and several elegies to Stagnelius. Two years later he published *Sorrow and the Star,* and two years after that, *Buy the Blind Man's Song.* He is speaking of the yellow-and-black armband worn by blind persons. His World War II book was called *Non Serviam.* He hated the Swedish welfare state. In general, he thought social movements were meaningless. He said, "When you have come as far as I have in meaninglessness / every word becomes interesting again."

Ekelöf loved seclusion. Apparently he bought a fine house for his wife in a well-developed park, but he himself lived in a tiny trailer house parked near the main door. During the last ten years of his life, he received many prizes and honorary awards. He died in Stockholm in 1968.

QUESTIONNAIRE

What do you consider your mission in life?
I am an absolutely useless human being.
What are your political convictions?
What we have now is fine. The opposition
to what we have now is fine. One ought to be
able to imagine a third — but what?
Your opinion on religion, if any?
The same as my opinion on music, namely only
he who is truly unmusical can be musical.
What do you look for in people? My relationships
have unfortunately little or no constancy.
What do you look for in literature? Philosophic depth?
Breadth or height? Epic? Lyric?
I look for the perfect circle.
What is the most beautiful thing you know of?
Birds in the cemeteries, butterflies on battlefields,
something in between. I really don't know.
Your favorite hobby? I have no hobby.
Your favorite sin? Onanism.
And to conclude (as briefly as possible):
Why do you write?
I have nothing else to do. Emma Wright?
You make puns, also?
I do make puns, yes.

from ÉTUDES

3

Each person is a world, peopled
by blind creatures in dim revolt
against the I, the king, who rules them.
In each soul thousands of souls are imprisoned,
in each world thousands of worlds are hidden
and these blind and lower worlds
are real and living, though not full-born,
as truly as I am real. And we kings
and barons of the thousand potential creatures within us
are citizens ourselves, imprisoned
in some larger creature, whose ego and nature
we understand as little as our master
his master. From their death and their love
our own feelings have received a coloring.

As when a great liner passes by
far out below the horizon where the sea lies
so still at dusk. And we know nothing of it
until a swell reaches us on the shore,
first one, then one more, and then many
washing and breaking until it all goes back
as before. Yet it is all changed.

So we shadows are seized by a strange unrest
when something tells us that people have left,
that some of the possible creatures have gotten free.

MONOLOGUE WITH ITS WIFE

Take two extra-old cabinet ministers and overtake them on the
    North Sea
Provide each of them with a comet in the rear
Seven comets each!
Send a wire:
If the city of Trondheim takes them in it will be bombed
If the suet field allows them to escape it will be bombed
Now you have to signal:
Larger ships approaching
Don't you see, there in the radio! Larger ships
in converging path. Send a warning!
All small strawberry boats shall be ordered to go into the shore and
    lie down

—Come and help me. I am disappearing.
The god is in the process of transforming me, the one in the corner
    over there (whispering)

from VARIATIONS

5

I believe in the solitary person,
in the man who walks about alone,
and does not run like a dog back to his own scent,
and does not run like a wolf away from human scent:
At once human and anti-human.

How to reach community?
Avoid the upper and the outer road:
What is herdlike in others is herdlike also in you.
Take the lower and inward road!
What is ground in you is ground also in others.

Hard to get into the habit of yourself.
Hard to get out of the habit of yourself.

He who does it shall never be deserted anyway.
He who does it shall remain loyal anyway.
The impractical is the only thing practical
in the long run.

6

There exists something that fits nowhere
and yet is in no way remarkable
and yet is decisive
and yet is outside it all.
There exists something which is noticed just when it is not noticeable
(like silence)
and is not noticed just when it becomes noticeable
for then it is mistaken (like silence) for something else.

See the waves under the sky. Storm is surface
and storm our way of seeing.
(What do I care for the waves or the seventh wave.)
There is an emptiness between the waves:
Look at the sea. Look at the stones of the field.
There is an emptiness between the stones:
They did not break loose—they did not throw themselves here,
They lie there and exist—a part of the rock sheath.
So make yourself heavy—make use of your dead weight,
let it break you, let it throw you, fall down,
let it leave you shipwrecked on the rock!
(What do I care about the rock.)

There are universes, suns, and atoms.
There is a knowledge, carefully built on strong points.
There is a knowledge, unprotected, built on insecure emptiness.
There is an emptiness between universes, suns, and atoms.
(What do I care about universes, suns, and atoms.)
There is an odd viewpoint on everything
in this double life.

There is peace beyond all.
There is peace behind all.
There is peace inside all.

Concealed in the hand.
Concealed in the pen.
Concealed in the ink.
I feel peace everywhere.
I smell peace behind everything.
I see and hear peace inside everything,
monotonous peace beyond everything.
(What do I care about peace.)

from THE SWAN

1

I heard wild geese over the hospital grounds
where many pale people walk back and forth
—one morning in a daze
I heard them! I hear them!
I dreamt I heard—

And nevertheless I did hear them!

Here endless walks circle about
around bottomless dams
Here the days all reflect
one monotonous day
at the slightest touch
beautiful blossoms close
their strange petals—

The woman on a nurse's arm
she screams incessantly:
Hell Devil Hell
—is led home
hurriedly . . .
Dusk has come
over the salmon-colored buildings
and outside the wall
an anemic blush over endless suburbs
of identical houses
with some vegetable beds steaming as if in spring between . . .

They are burning twigs and leaves:
It is fall
and the vegetable beds are attacked by worm-eaten cabbages
and bare flowers—

I heard wild geese over the hospital grounds
one autumnlike spring morning
I heard wild geese one morning
one springautumn morning
trumpeting—

To the north? To the south?
To the north! To the north!
Far from here—

A freshness lives deep in me
which no one can take from me
not even I myself—

IF YOU ASK ME WHERE I LIVE

If you ask me where I live
I live right here behind the mountain
It's a long way off but I am near
I live in another world
but you live there also
That world is everywhere even if it is as rare as helium
Why do you ask for an airship to bear you off?
Ask instead for a filter for carbon dioxide
a filter for hydrogen, for nitrogen, and other gases
Ask for a filter for all these things that separate us from one another
a filter for life
You say you can hardly breathe?
Well, who do you think *can* breathe?
For the most part we take it however with equanimity
A wise man has said:
"It was so dark I could barely see the stars"
He just meant that it was night

ISSA

ISSA IS THE most playful of the haiku poets. He is always making jokes with frogs, speaking to crickets he notices in bed with him: "Cricket, be careful. I am rolling over." Early in his life, he became a Pure Land Buddhist. The Pure Land group was created as a kind of alternative or rebuke to Rinzai Zen, for mentorship in which a rich cultural training was required. Many intricate disciplines around warriorhood came into Rinzai as well. When the Pure Land Buddhist sect was developed in the eleventh century, ordinary farmers could join it, as well as tradespeople and thieves. The sect fit Issa perfectly. At that time, windowpanes were made of paper. Issa notices a tear in his window paper. He says, "It's true I have a tear—but through it I can see the Milky Way." He stood up for or with the poor. He said, "Sparrows, look out! Big-ass horse is coming through!" His poems are wonderfully lighthearted. They show that astonishing observation of details of nature that we associate with Thoreau in his best prose or Tu Fu in his description of the battle between chickens and ants, or William Carlos Williams in some of his spring and fall poems.

Issa's task was to return the haiku to the rich outdoor place where Basho had left it a hundred years earlier. Basho said, "You can learn about the pine only from the pine, and about bamboo only from bamboo." It's not that Basho wanted more pine and less self, but he wanted more pine and more pine-self. Tiny details seen with a high and serious intent was an ideal for both poets.

———

ISSA was born Yatoro Kobayashi in 1763 in a small mountain village in central Japan, the eldest son of a farm family. His father evidently loved writing haiku, and left several good haiku behind. When Issa was two, his mother died, but he always felt near to her. One of his poems could be translated as: "Whenever I see the ocean, I see my mother's face." His grandfather brought Issa up, and he apparently received some schooling from a haiku poet in the neighborhood. When he was seven, his father married again, and now he fell on hard times. The son of the new marriage was favored, and Issa was apparently whipped a hundred times a day.

When he was thirteen, he left home and went to live in what is now Tokyo. There he joined a group of poets who were trying to revive the sober, moving style in which Basho wrote. When he was twenty-seven he went back to his village and was reconciled with his father. Two years later, he adopted the pen name Issa, which means "a cup of tea." This simple pen name fit well with the Pure Land school.

He soon began to take a series of long walking trips, much as Basho had done a century earlier, and he kept up this habit for the next ten years. He would write haiku about what happened each day. The most famous of those collections is *The Year of My Life,* which was well translated a few years ago by Nobuyuki Yuasa, who was aware that a walking trip for Basho was a discipline in solitude and a mode of renunciation. But for Issa, this tended to bond him more closely to human beings than he might have in everyday life.

After his father died, Issa returned and settled in his native village — in fact in the house in which he was born. By then he was fifty-one. He married a young woman who was about twenty-seven, and they had a child who died shortly after birth. The next child died as well. At last a daughter, Sato, was born. Issa had a great love for her, though he recognized that this attachment was not quite in line with Buddhism. When she died, he said,

I know this world
is a drop of dew—
and still . . . still . . .

Some months later, he wrote another haiku about her:

Last night I dreamt
my daughter lifted
a melon to her cheek.

Several of the poems that are included here are from *The Year of My Life,* which is set in 1819. He faced many griefs that year, and after that, other disasters followed. Two more babies died, then his wife. He married two more times; nothing worked. And in 1827, his house burned down. By that time Issa was ill, and the next day he was moved to a kind of granary in which snow came in through the cracks in the wall. When he died, his death poem was found under his pillow:

This snow on the bed quilt—
this too
is from the Pure Land.

Insects, why cry?
We all go
that way.

Now listen, you watermelons —
if any thieves come —
turn into frogs!

Leaping for the river, the frog
said, "Excuse
me for going first!"

The night is so long,
Yes, the night is so long;
Buddha is great!

Morning glories, yes—
but in the faces of men
there are flaws.

Lanky frog, hold
your ground! Issa
is coming!

This line of black ants—
Maybe it goes all the way back
to that white cloud!

The old dog bends his head listening . . .
I guess the singing
of the earthworms gets to him.

Cricket, be
careful! I'm rolling
over!

THE PIGEON MAKES HIS REQUEST

Since it's spring and raining,
could we have a little different expression,
oh owl?

FEDERICO GARCÍA LORCA

LORCA IS THE genius of geniuses: no one like him has ever been
born, and no one like him will ever be born again. He arrives in the
world with the full knowledge that every particle in the universe is
searching:

> The rose
> was not searching for the sunrise:
> almost eternal on its branch,
> it was searching for something else.

Those readers whose soul can vibrate like an instrument made of
old wood fall in love with him during the first poem, and become
faithful lovers.

> The rose
> was not searching for darkness or science:
> borderline of flesh and dream,
> it was searching for something else.

Even a genius is not searching for genius.

> The rose
> was not searching for the rose.
> Motionless in the sky
> it was searching for something else.

Lorca's poetry inherited much delicacy from medieval Arabic-Andalusian poetry, but his immediate spiritual father was Juan Ramón Jiménez. Jiménez's love of silence, his love of perfection, his gaiety of soul was famous in Madrid.

If we read Lorca and Jiménez carefully, we can sense the subtle nature of the soul ground from which prophetic poetry rises. It is a ground cultivated in silence behind garden walls, shrewdly protected, loving the perfections of high art, an art that fights for the values of the feminine and reverie and the soul:

> When the moon sails out
> the sea covers the earth
> and the heart feels it is
> a little island in the infinite.

He says that everyone is looking for his or her voice, because only your own voice can do it.

> The small boy is looking for his voice.
> (The King of the Crickets had it.)
> The boy was looking
> in a drop of water for his voice.

I follow Lorca's images with amazement; and as soon as I have caught up to one of them and taken it in, I see only his coattails. He was not waiting for us; he has gone on far ahead.

> All I want is a single hand,
> A wounded hand if that is possible.
> All I want is a single hand
> Even if I have no bed for a thousand nights.

He inherited from the gypsy flamenco singers, whom he loved, the delicate dance before pure death that a bullfighter dances. He loved the taunting of death by those who had lost much to him already, and would soon lose more, lose all, as Mary did, as Joseph and Jesus did.

FEDERICO GARCÍA LORCA was born in 1898 in a small Andalusian town west of Granada. The family established a house in the city itself when Federico was eleven. You can still see that house in Granada, in the center of a grove of trees; you can still see the piano on which he left his music when he was taken off to be shot. How near was the house, and often the grove is filled with schoolchildren come to visit that sweet place!

As an adolescent, he participated in the rich cultural life around the Café Alameda in Granada. When he was twenty, his parents agreed to enroll him in the famous Residence de Estudiantes in Madrid, a place modeled on Oxford and Cambridge, based on liberal ideas. There he heard Claudel, Valéry, Cendrars, Marinetti, Wanda Landowska, and became close friends with Rafael Alberti, Salvador Dalí, and Luis Buñuel. Juan Ramón Jiménez became a sort of mentor to him. Lorca published *Book of Poems* in 1921, along with other early books, and the *Gypsy Ballads* in 1927.

He loved flamenco or Cante Jondo music; he also wrote puppet plays and farces. Becoming a bit tired of his reputation as a "gypsy poet," he left Spain. With a friend he traveled to New York in June of 1929, where he took some English classes at Columbia University. There he saw the full power of the Depression. He saw the full collision of the feeling life of provincial Granada and the brutality of what would become global capitalism. His response was the book he wrote, later printed as *Poet in New York,* still the greatest poem about New York. After he returned to Spain, he wrote a number of ghazals giving honor to the love poetry of the Arabs. He also organized a traveling theater troupe, so as to be closer to the Spanish people. He was fearful of attack because of his homosexuality, and his fears turned out to be justified. In August of 1936, the fascists had become active in Granada, and he was taken from his house and shot. So his life ended at thirty-eight.

QUESTIONS

A parliament of grasshoppers is in the field.
What do you say, Marcus Aurelius,
about these old philosophers of the prairie?
Your thought is so full of poverty!

The waters of the river move slowly.
Oh Socrates! What do you see
in the water moving toward its bitter death?
Your faith is full of poverty and sad!

The leaves of the roses fall in the mud.
Oh sweet John of God!
What do you see in these magnificent petals?
Your heart is tiny!

THE BOY UNABLE TO SPEAK

The small boy is looking for his voice.
(The King of the Crickets had it.)
The boy was looking
in a drop of water for his voice.

I don't want the voice to speak with;
I will make a ring from it
that my silence will wear
on its little finger.

The small boy was looking
in a drop of water for his voice.

(Far away the captured voice
was getting dressed up like a cricket.)

SONG OF THE RIDER

Córdoba.
Distant and alone.

Black pony, full moon,
and olives inside my saddlebag.
Though I know the roads well,
I will never arrive at Córdoba.

Over the low plains, over the winds,
black pony, red moon.
Death is looking down at me
from the towers of Córdoba.

What a long road this is!
What a brave horse I have!
Death is looking for me
before I get to Córdoba!

Córdoba.
Distant and alone.

MALAGUENA

Death
is entering and leaving
the tavern.

Black horses and sinister
people are riding
over the deep roads
of the guitar.

There is an odor of salt
and the blood of women
in the feverish spice-plants
by the sea.

Death
is entering and leaving
the tavern,
death
leaving and entering.

THE QUARREL
For Rafael Méndez

The Albacete knives, magnificent
with stranger-blood,
flash like fishes
on the gully slope.
Light crisp as a playing
card snips out of bitter
green the profiles of riders
and maddened horses.
Two old women in an olive
tree are sobbing.
The bull of the quarrel
is rising up the walls.
Black angels arrived
with handkerchiefs and snow water.
Angels with immense wings
like Albacete knives.
Juan Antonio from Montilla
rolls dead down the hill,
his body covered with lilies,
a pomegranate on his temples.
He is riding now on the cross of fire,
on the highway of death.

*

The State Police and the judge
come along through the olive grove.
From the earth loosed blood moans
the silent folk song of the snake.
"Well, Your Honor, you see,

it's the same old business —
four Romans are dead
and five Carthaginians."

*

Dusk that the fig trees and the
hot whispers have made hysterical
faints and falls on the bloody
thighs of the riders,
and black angels went on flying
through the failing light,
angels with long hair,
and hearts of olive oil.

THAMAR AND AMNON
For Alfonso García-Valdecasas

The moon turns in the sky
above the dry fields
and the summer plants
rumors of tiger and flame.
Nerves of metal
resonated over the roofs.
Bleatings made of wool
arrived on curly winds.
The earth lies covered
with scarred-over wounds,
or shaken by the sharp
burnings of white stars.

*

Thamar was dreaming of
birds in her throat.
She heard frost tambourines
and moon-covered zithers.
Her nakedness on the roof,
a palm pointing north,
asks for snowflakes at her stomach,
and hailstones at her shoulders.
Thamar was there singing
naked on the rooftop.

*

Huddled near her feet
five frozen doves.
Amnon, lithe and firm,
watched her from his tower.
His genitals were like surf,

and his beard swaying.
Her luminous nakedness
stretched out on the terrace,
her teeth sound like an arrow
that has just hit its mark.
Amnon was looking over
at the round and heavy moon,
and he saw there the hard
breasts of his sister.

*

At three-thirty Amnon
threw himself on his bed.
The hundred wings in his eyes
disturbed the whole room.
The moonlight, massive, buries
towns under dark sand,
or opens a mortal coral
of dahlias and roses.
Underground water oppressed
breaks its silence in jars.
The cobra is singing on the tree,
stretched out on the mosses.
Amnon groans from the fresh
sheets of his bed.
An ivy of icy fever
covers his burning body.
Thamar walked silently
into the silence of his bedroom,
the color of blood and Danube
troubled with far-off footprints.
"Thamar, put out my eyes
with your piercing dawn.
The threads of my blood

are weaving the folds on your dress."
"Leave me be, brother.
Your kisses are wasps
on my shoulder, and winds blowing
in a double twirling of flutes."
"Thamar, I hear two fishes
calling me from your steep breasts,
and the sound of closed rosebuds
in the tips of your fingers."

*

The hundred horses of the king
neigh together in the courtyard.
The sun in buckets fought
the slenderness of the vine.
Now he takes her by the hair,
now he rips her dress.
Warm corals start drawing
rivulets on a blond country.

*

What screams are heard now
lifting above the houses!
What a thicket of knives,
and cloaks torn up!
Slaves keep going up
the sad stairs and back down.
Pistons and thighs play
under the motionless clouds.
Standing around Thamar
gypsy virgins give cries,
others gather up the drops
of her murdered flower.
White fabrics slowly turn red
in the locked bedrooms.

At first whisper of warm dawn
fish turn back into tendrils.

*

    The raper, Amnon, flees,
wild, on his horse.
Negroes shoot arrows
at him from the parapets.
When the beat of the four hoofs
became four fading chords,
David took a scissors
and cut the strings of his harp.

from POET IN NEW YORK

While the Chinaman was crying on the roof
without finding the nakedness of his wife,
and the bank president was watching the pressure gauge
that measures the remorseless silence of money,
the black mask was arriving at Wall Street.

This vault that makes the eyes turn yellow
is not an odd place for dancing.
There is a wire stretched from the Sphinx to the safety deposit box
that passes through the heart of all poor children.
The primitive energy is dancing with the machine energy,
in their frenzy wholly ignorant of the original light.
Because if the wheel forgets its formula,
it might as well sing naked with the herds of horses;
and if a flame burns up the frozen plains
the sky will have to run away from the roar of the windows.

This place is a good place for dancing, I say this truth,
the black mask will dance between columns of blood and numbers,
between downpours of gold and groans of unemployed workers
who will go howling, dark night, through your time without stars.
O savage North America! shameless! savage,
stretched out on the frontier of the snow!

RUN-DOWN CHURCH
(Ballad of the First World War)

    I had a son and his name was John.
I had a son.
He disappeared into the arches one Friday of All Souls.
I saw him playing on the highest steps of the Mass
throwing a little tin pail at the heart of the priest.
I knocked on the coffin. My son! My son! My son!
I drew out a chicken foot from behind the moon and then
I understood that my daughter was a fish
down which the carts vanish.
I had a daughter.
I had a fish dead under the ashes of the incense burner.
I had an ocean. Of what? Good Lord! An ocean!
I went up to ring the bells but the fruit was all wormy
and the blackened match-ends
were eating the spring wheat.
I saw a stork of alcohol you could see through
shaving the black heads of the dying soldiers
and I saw the rubber booths
where the goblets full of tears were whirling.
In the anemones of the offertory I will find you, my love!
when the priest with his strong arms raises up the mule and the ox
to scare the nighttime toads that roam in the icy landscapes of the
    chalice.
I had a son who was a giant,
but the dead are stronger and know how to gobble down pieces of
    the sky.
If my son had only been a bear,
I wouldn't fear the secrecy of the crocodiles
and I wouldn't have seen the ocean roped to the trees

to be raped and wounded by the mobs from the regiment.

If my son had only been a bear!

I'll roll myself in this rough canvas so as not to feel the chill of the
mosses.

I know very well they will give me a sleeve or a necktie,

but in the innermost part of the Mass I'll smash the rudder and then

the insanity of the penguins and seagulls will come to the rock

and then they will make the people sleeping and the people singing on
the street corners say:

he had a son.

A son! A son! A son

and it was no one else's, because it was his son!

His son! His son! His son!

LITTLE INFINITE POEM
For Luis Cardoza y Aragón

To take the wrong road
is to arrive at the snow
and to arrive at the snow
is to get down on all fours for twenty centuries and eat the grasses of
   the cemeteries.

To take the wrong road
is to arrive at a woman,
woman who isn't afraid of light,
woman who murders two roosters in one second,
light which isn't afraid of roosters,
and roosters who don't know how to sing on top of the snow.

But if the snow truly takes the wrong road,
then it might meet the southern wind,
and since the air cares nothing for groans,
we will have to get down on all fours again and eat the grasses of the
   cemeteries.

I saw two mournful wheatheads made of wax
burying a countryside of volcanoes;
and I saw two insane little boys who wept as they leaned on a mur-
   derer's eyeballs.

But two has never been a number—
because it's only an anguish and its shadow,
it's only a guitar where love feels how hopeless it is,
it's the proof of someone else's infinity,
and the walls around a dead man,

and the scourging of a new resurrection that will never end.
Dead people hate the number two,
but the number two makes women drop off to sleep,
and since women are afraid of light,
light shudders when it has to face the roosters,
and since all roosters know is how to fly over the snow
we will have to get down on all fours and eat the grasses of the ceme-
  teries forever.

JANUARY 10, 1930. NEW YORK.

NEW YORK
(*Office and Attack*)

To Fernando Vela

 Beneath all the statistics
there is a drop of duck's blood.
Beneath all the columns
there is a drop of sailor's blood.
Beneath all the totals, a river of warm blood;
a river that goes singing
past the bedrooms of the suburbs,
and the river is silver, cement, or wind
in the lying daybreak of New York.
The mountains exist, I know that.
And the lenses ground for wisdom,
I know that. But I have not come to see the sky.
I have come to see the stormy blood,
the blood that sweeps the machines to the waterfalls,
and the spirit on the cobra's tongue.
Every day they kill in New York
ducks, four million,
pigs, five million,
pigeons, two thousand, for the enjoyment of dying men,
cows, one million,
lambs, one million,
roosters, two million
who turn the sky to small splinters.
You may as well sob filing a razor blade
or assassinate dogs in the hallucinated foxhunts,
as try to stop in the dawnlight
the endless trains carrying milk,

the endless trains carrying blood,
and the trains carrying roses in chains
for those in the field of perfume.
The ducks and the pigeons
and the hogs and the lambs
lay their drops of blood down
underneath all the statistics;
and the terrible bawling of the packed-in cattle
fills the valley with suffering
where the Hudson is getting drunk on its oil.
I attack all those persons
who know nothing of the other half,
the half who cannot be saved,
who raise their cement mountains
in which the hearts of the small
animals no one thinks of are beating,
and from which we will all fall
during the final holiday of the drills.
I spit in your face.
The other half hears me,
as they go on eating, urinating, flying in their purity
like the children of the janitors
who carry delicate sticks
to the holes where the antennas
of the insects are rusting.
This is not hell, it is a street.
This is not death, it is a fruit stand.
There is a whole world of crushed rivers and unachievable distances
in the paw of a cat crushed by a car,
and I hear the song of the worm
in the heart of so many girls.
Rust, rotting, trembling earth.
And you are earth, swimming through the figures of the office.

What shall I do, set my landscapes in order?
Set in place the lovers who will afterwards be photographs,
who will be bits of wood and mouthfuls of blood?
No, I won't; I attack,
I attack the conspiring
of these empty offices
that will not broadcast the sufferings,
that rub out the plans of the forest,
and I offer myself to be eaten by the packed-up cattle
when their mooing fills the valley
where the Hudson is getting drunk on its oil.

SONG OF THE CUBAN BLACKS

When the full moon comes
I'll go to Santiago in Cuba.
I'll go to Santiago
in a carriage of black water.
I'll go to Santiago.
Palm-thatching will start to sing.
I'll go to Santiago.
When the palm trees want to turn into storks,
I'll go to Santiago.
When the banana trees want to turn into jellyfish,
I'll go to Santiago.
With the golden head of Fonseca.
I'll go to Santiago.
And with the rose of Romeo and Juliet
I'll go to Santiago.
Oh Cuba! Oh rhythm of dry seeds!
I'll go to Santiago.
Oh warm waist, and a drop of wood!
I'll go to Santiago.
Harp of living trees. Crocodile. Tobacco blossom!
I'll go to Santiago.
I always said I would go to Santiago
in a carriage of black water.
I'll go to Santiago.
Wind and alcohol in the wheels,
I'll go to Santiago.
My coral in the darkness,
I'll go to Santiago.
The ocean drowned in the sand,

I'll go to Santiago.
White head and dead fruit,
I'll go to Santiago.
Oh wonderful freshness of the cane fields!
Oh Cuba! Arc of sighs and mud!
I'll go to Santiago.

GHAZAL OF THE DARK DEATH

I want to sleep the sleep of the apples,
I want to get far away from the busyness of the cemeteries.
I want to sleep the sleep of that child
who longed to cut his heart open far out at sea.

I don't want them to tell me again how the corpse keeps all its blood,
how the decaying mouth goes on begging for water.
I'd rather not hear about the torture sessions the grass arranges for
nor about how the moon does all its work before dawn
with its snakelike nose.

I want to sleep for half a second,
a second, a minute, a century,
but I want everyone to know that I am still alive,
that I have a golden manger inside my lips,
that I am the little friend of the west wind,
that I am the elephantine shadow of my own tears.

When it's dawn just throw some sort of cloth over me
because I know dawn will toss fistfuls of ants at me,
and pour a little hard water over my shoes
so that the scorpion claws of the dawn will slip off.

Because I want to sleep the sleep of the apples,
and learn a mournful song that will clean all earth away from me,
because I want to live with that shadowy child
who longed to cut his heart open far out at sea.

GHAZAL OF THE TERRIFYING PRESENCE

I want the water to go on without its bed.
And the wind to go on without its mountain passes.

I want the night to go on without its eyes
and my heart without its golden petals;

If the oxen could only talk with the big leaves
and the angleworm would die from too much darkness;

I want the teeth in the skull to shine
and the yellowish tints to drown the silk.

I can see the night in its duel, wounded
and wrestling, tangled with noon.

I fight against a sunset of green poison,
and those broken arches where time is suffering.

But don't let the light fall on your clear and naked body
like a cactus black and open in the reeds.

Leave me in the anguish of the darkened planets,
but do not let me see your pure waist.

CASIDA OF THE ROSE

The rose
was not searching for the sunrise:
almost eternal on its branch,
it was searching for something else.

The rose
was not searching for darkness or science:
borderline of flesh and dream,
it was searching for something else.

The rose
was not searching for the rose.
Motionless in the sky
it was searching for something else.

OLAV H. HAUGE

OLAV H. HAUGE'S flavor is persistent, like the taste of persimmons which we can never forget. His poems are as nourishing as an old apple that a goat has found in the orchard. He has much to give, and he gives it in small spoonfuls, as nurses give medicine. Everywhere in the daylight of his work, you see tiny experiences being valued.

> Midwinter. Snow.
> I gave the birds a piece of bread.
> And it didn't affect my sleep.

He loved to honor culture, and he honored it more than many classics professors do. People in his neighborhood felt a little fear when they entered his small, book-filled house. He was liable to pull down a fat volume, printed in Oxford, and say, "No doubt you've read this?" Very few people in town had read it, but there wasn't a trace of scorn in his question. He loved the book so much he thought it quite possible that you knew it too.

What is it like to spend your whole life on a farm with no support from your family or from the community? It would be lonely, something like walking in a marsh in the middle of the woods.

> It is the roots from all the trees that have died
> out here, that's how you can walk
> safely over the soft places.

One would have to realize that the old Chinese poets have lived this sort of life before you; they wrote poems; they didn't die of fear. Hauge was able to compare himself to a drowned person he once heard about.

> That cold person
> who drowned himself here once
> helps hold up your frail boat.
> He, really crazy, trusted his life
> to water and eternity.

If you have a tiny farm, you need to love poetry more than the farm. If you sell apples, you need to love poetry more than the apples. It's good to settle down somewhere and to love poetry more than that.

Lewis Hyde in his great book called *The Gift* discusses the nature of the old pre-commercial gift-giving society. The economy of scarcity, he says, is always associated with gift-giving. Olav H. Hauge lived in a gift-giving, pre-communal society all of his life. The richness in his small house lay in the handmade spoons and bowls, the wooden reading chair, and the bookcases to which the best poetry from many continents had found its way.

OLAV H. HAUGE was born in 1908 in Ulvik, a tiny settlement in Hardanger north of Utne, and he died there eighty years later. As a typical younger son in a traditional Norwegian family, he received virtually no land. The older brother gets the main farm, and Olav lived all his life on what he could produce from three acres of ground. During his late twenties, he spent some time in a mental institution. He married for the first time at sixty-five, to the Norwegian artist Bodil Cappelen, who had met him at one of his rare poetry readings. He settled into married life very well, and his house became considerably cheerier. He died in the old way; no real evidence of disease was present. He simply didn't eat for ten days and so he died. People who attended his funeral, which took place at a church down in the valley where he had been baptized as a child, described a service full of feeling and gratitude. A horse-drawn wagon carried his body back up the mountain after the service. Everyone noticed a small colt that ran happily alongside its mother and the coffin all the way back up.

MIDWINTER. SNOW.

Midwinter. Snow.
I gave the birds a piece of bread.
And it didn't affect my sleep.

LOOKING AT AN OLD MIRROR

The front a mirror.
The back a picture of the Garden of Eden.

A strange find
of the old master of glass.

DON'T COME TO ME
WITH THE ENTIRE TRUTH

Don't come to me with the entire truth.
Don't bring the ocean if I feel thirsty,
nor heaven if I ask for light;
but bring a hint, some dew, a particle,
as birds carry only drops away from water,
and the wind a grain of salt.

HARVEST TIME

These calm days of September with their sun.
It's time to harvest. There are still clumps
of cranberries in the woods, reddening rosehips
by the stone walls, hazelnuts coming loose,
and clusters of black berries shine in the bushes;
thrushes look around for the last currants
and wasps fasten on to the sweetening plums.
I set the ladder aside at dusk, and hang
my basket up in the shed. The glaciers
all have a thin sprinkling of new snow. In bed
I hear the brisling fishermen start their motors
and go out. They'll pass the whole night
gliding over the fjord behind their powerful searchlights.

LEAF HUTS AND SNOW HOUSES

These poems don't amount
to much, just
some words thrown together
at random.
And still
to me
there's something good
in making them, it's
as if I have in them for a little
while a house.
I think of playhouses
made of branches we built
when we were children:
to crawl into them, sit
listening to the rain,
in a wild place alone,
feel the drops of rain on your nose
and in your hair—
or snow houses at Christmas,
crawl in and close it after
with a sack,
light a candle, be there
through the long chill evenings.

EVENING CLOUDS

Clouds are arriving now
With greetings from
Distant coasts;
It's been a while since
They sent a message to me.
You shy pink
High on the evening sky—
It's probably for
Someone else.
Well, there's still
Some hope left
In the world.

ACROSS THE SWAMP

It is the roots from all the trees that have died
out here, that's how you can walk
safely over the soft places.
Roots like these keep their firmness, it's possible
they've lain here for centuries.
And there is still some dark remains
of them under the moss.
They are still in the world and hold
you up so you can make it over.
And when you push out into the mountain lake, high
up, you feel how the memory
of that cold person
who drowned himself here once
helps hold up your frail boat.
He, really crazy, trusted his life
to water and eternity.

I STAND HERE, D'YA UNDERSTAND

I stand here, d'ya understand.
I stood here last year too, d'ya understand.
I am going to stand here too, d'ya understand.
I take it too, d'ya understand.
There's something you don't know, d'ya understand.
You just got here, d'ya understand.
How long are we to stand here?
We have to eat too, d'ya understand.
I stand when I eat too, I do that, d'ya understand,
and throw the plates at the wall.
We have to rest too, d'ya understand.
We have to piss and shit too, d'ya understand.
How long are we to stand here?
I stand all right, d'ya understand.
I take it too, d'ya understand.
I'm going to stand here, d'ya understand.

THE BIG SCALES

It is the old-time weights
That are the significant things
In the weighing room
(Along with myself).
That's why they've gotten their spot
In the middle of the floor—it is
They who
Weigh and decide
What the freight charge will be.
I have a good sense
When I handle sacks and crates of apples
How heavy they are,
But they have to go onto the scales
So the scales can have their opinion.
We bargain—the two of us;
I add weights;
We mostly reach
Agreement—they tip,
I nod,
And we both say,
"That's it."—We
Don't bother much with ounces.
The scales are rusted, and I
Am stiff in my back
And that's OK, the weights are lighter
Than the thoughts I am weighing.
Sometimes I notice that people have doubts
If my figures are right.
People are odd.
If they sell something

They want it heavy;
If they ship it
They want it light.
A judge came here one day;
He also brooded about scales, probably
Thinking what things he
Has to weigh.
"These aren't pharmacist's scales," I said,
But I really was remembering scales I once
Saw at a goldsmith shop.
He weighed gold dust
Using tweezers.
I've thoughts also of what
A judge has to weigh:
Right and wrong,
Sentences and fines,
Life and destiny.
Who checks over
Those weights,
And those scales?

IT IS THAT DREAM

It's that dream we carry with us
That something wonderful will happen,
That it has to happen,
That time will open,
That the heart will open,
That doors will open,
That the mountains will open,
That wells will leap up,
That the dream will open,
That one morning we'll slip in
To a harbor that we've never known.

THE DREAM

Let us slip into
Sleep, into
The calm dream,
Just slip in—two bits
Of raw dough in the
Good oven
That we call night,
And so to awake
In the morning as
Two sound
Golden loaves!

THE CARPET

Weave a carpet for me, Bodil,
weave it from dreams and visions,
weave it out of wind,
so that I, like a Bedouin, can
roll it out when I pray,
pull it around me
when I sleep,
and then every morning cry out,
"Table, set yourself!"
Weave it
for a cape in the cold weather,
and a sail
for my boat!
One day I will sit down on the carpet
and sail away on it
to another world.

HARRY MARTINSON

HARRY MARTINSON BELONGS to the generation of John Steinbeck, Tillie Olsen, and Kenneth Rexroth. He was brought up in the Swedish southeast, and remembers how that childhood was:

> And other insignificant things happened at the same time.
> The kicksled broke a thin leg
> and we rolled around like food baskets in snow on the zinc-gray ice.
>
> Clary—you and I.
> We sat down deep in the snowy bushes by the shore,
> we pissed in the snow,
> and laughed like mad about it, as children do.
> There was a starvation winter, with rickets,
> and epidemics going all around the lake.

It's clear from the nakedness of his poems that for years he walked around the world in charge of his own skin, and of little more.

His poems have a curious and luminous grace of language. The poems slip on through their own words like a ship cutting through a quiet sea. Everything feels alive, fragrant, resilient, like seaweed underwater. In Swedish his poems feel a little like Lawrence in "Bavarian Gentians." A good Martinson poem never closes with a snap. It is like a tunnel that is open at both ends.

His poems have something that Lawrence's do not, as well. We feel in his work an experience of modern commerce possible only to one who has made his living in it. Martinson's work as a seaman brought him in touch not only with the romantic body of the sea, as similar work did for Gary Snyder, but also with the stiff skeletal will of commerce. When Martinson talks of trade, he drops all thought of brotherhood; he knows it cannot be reformed. Meeting Ogden Armour's yacht is like shaking hands with a rock.

> In the latitude of the Balearic Islands
> we sighted Ogden Armour's yacht.
> This cargo ship is part of his fleet, as you know,
> he has five slaughterhouses in Chicago,
> and eight packing plants near La Plata.
> He put his telescope to his eye and no doubt said,
> "Oh Christ! It's nothing but my old cattleboat, the *Chattanooga*."
> We dipped the flag and all the cows started in mooing
> like a thousand hoarse sirens over the endless ocean.

Often Martinson's poems, by their sheer grace, shoot into the future and become prophetic. He begins to become aware of a certain flatness becoming prevalent in the West. What will happen when there is no more "undiscovered" wilderness? The world will gradually lose its inwardness; people will cry out for new worlds, they will look for a new world in the stars. The old Scandinavians found something wild in their trolls, in "the weird people" who would occasionally steal a daughter or a son. All that will be gone. We'll have flatness, a form of forgetfulness that is associated with repetitive motions. Even the demons will be flat. It is already happening:

> Demons flatter than stingrays
> swept above the plains of death,
> flock after flock of demons went abreast, in ranks, and parallel
> through Hades.

And the dead who are victims of flat evil—what will their afterlife be like? They will be received after death

> with no comfort from a high place
> or support from a low place,
> received without dignity,
> received without a rising,
> received without any of the standards of eternity.
> Their cries are met only by mockery
> on the flat fields of evil.

HARRY MARTINSON was born in 1904 in southeastern Sweden. His father died when he was six, and his mother emigrated to the United States, leaving the children in the parish. Martinson ran away from various schools, and finally signed on as a seaman when he was sixteen. He spent six years working as a deckhand or stoker on fourteen different ships, visiting many ports of the world. He returned home in 1926, published his first collection of poems, soon married, and established his credentials as a travel writer through two books of prose. He published three books of essays in the thirties. He was invited in 1934 to the Soviet Writers' Congress in Moscow, and was appalled by its motto: "The writer is the engineer of the human soul." A few years later, he took part as a volunteer in the Finnish war against the Russians.

In his novel *The Road to Klockrike* in 1948, he praises the life of tramps, he encourages indolence. It reminds us of John Steinbeck's California stories. Later, he began a large cycle of poems, which was published at last in 1956 as *Aniara*. Its story takes place after the earth has become hopelessly ruined by radiation; the giant spaceship *Aniara* takes off for Mars; but after four years, all the passengers die, and the spaceship continues on. This epic fantasy had an enormous effect in

Sweden; it was made into an opera, etc. It has been translated several times into English. Meanwhile, his nature poems remained as fresh as the earliest ones.

In 1974, Martinson received the Nobel Prize. It turned out to be an unhappy event. Swedish critics felt ashamed of his countrified poems. They tended to disdain all nature poetry, and in newspapers, attacked him on all fronts. He called off the publication of a book of nature poems, and died in 1978.

NO NAME FOR IT

It's marvellous in winter to dance on the ice —
and to carry memories of the torches
that threw light on us so long ago
as they swayed back and forth in the north wind.

And other insignificant things happened at the same time.
The kicksled broke a thin leg
and we rolled around like food baskets in snow on the zinc-gray ice.

Clary — you and I.
We sat down deep in the snowy bushes by the shore,
we pissed in the snow,
and laughed like mad about it, as children do.
There was a starvation winter, with rickets,
and epidemics going all around the lake.

Clary — you had such impudent, beautiful eyes —
and you died before your breasts had begun to grow.

CREATION NIGHT

We met on the stone bridge,
the birches stood watch for us,
the river gleaming like an eel wound toward the sea.
We twisted together in order to create God,
there was a rustling in the grain,
and a wave shot out of the rye.

LIGHTHOUSE KEEPER

In the puffing gusty nights,
when the lighthouse sways under storm clouds,
and the sea with its burning eyes climbs on the rocks,
you sit silently, thinking—
about Liz—who betrayed you that time—
and the fated, howling longing that exiled you out here
in the storm-beaten Scilly Islands.
And you mumble something to yourself
during the long watches on stormy nights
while the beacon throws its light a hundred miles out in the storm.

MARCH EVENING

Winterspring, nightfall, thawing.
Boys have lit a candle in a snowball house.
For the man in the evening train that rattles past,
it is a red memory surrounded by gray time,
calling, calling, out of stark woods just waking up.
And the man who was traveling never got home,
his life stayed behind, held by that lantern and that hour.

THE CABLE SHIP

We fished up the Atlantic Cable one day between the Barbados and
    the Tortugas,
held up our lanterns
and put some rubber over the wound in its back,
latitude 15 degrees north, longitude 61 degrees west.
When we laid our ear down to the gnawed place
we could hear something humming inside the cable.

"It's some millionaires in Montreal and St. John
talking over the price of Cuban sugar, and ways to
reduce our wages," one of us said.

For a long time we stood there thinking, in a circle of lanterns,
we're all patient fishermen,
then we let the coated cable fall back
to its place in the sea.

COTTON

The day they strung the cable from America to Europe
they did a lot of singing.
The cable, the huge singing cable was put in use
and Europe said to America:
Give me three million tons of cotton!
And three million tons of cotton wandered over the ocean
and turned to cloth:
cloth with which one fascinated the savages of Senegambia,
and cotton wads, with which one killed them.
Raise your voice in song, sing
on all the Senegambic trading routes!
sing cotton!
cotton!

Yes, cotton, your descent on the earth like snow!
Your white peace for our dead bodies!
Your while anklelength gowns when we wander into heaven
saved in all the world's harbors by Booth's Jesus-like face.

Cotton, cotton, your snowfall:
wrapping the world in the fur of new necessities,
you shut us in, you blinded our eyes with your cloud.
At the mouth of the Trade River,
and on the wide oceans of markets and fairs,
cotton, we have met there
the laws of your flood,
the threat of your flood.

LETTER FROM A CATTLEBOAT

In the latitude of the Balearic Islands
we sighted Ogden Armour's yacht.
This cargo ship is part of his fleet, as you know,
he has five slaughterhouses in Chicago,
and eight packing plants near La Plata.
He put his telescope to his eye and no doubt said,
"Oh Christ! It's nothing but my old cattleboat, the *Chattanooga*."

We dipped the flag and all the cows started in mooing
like a thousand hoarse sirens over the endless ocean.
It was depressing,
and I felt like writing the whole thing off as: flesh praising flesh.

Shortly after we hit a heavy storm
and the cows, that have four stomachs, as you know,
had a bad time with seasickness.

ON THE CONGO

Our ship, the *Sea Smithy,* swerved out of the tradewinds
and began to creep up the Congo River.
Vines trailed along the deck like ropes.
We met the famous iron barges of the Congo,
whose hot steeldecks swarmed with Negroes from the tributaries.

They put their hands to their mouths
and shouted, "Go to hell" in a Bantu language.
We slid marveling and depressed through the tunnels of vegetation
and cook in his galley thought:
"now I am peeling potatoes in the middle of the Congo."

At night the *Sea Smithy*
goggled with its red eyes into the jungle,
an animal roared, a jungle rat plopped into the water,
a millet mortar coughed sharply,
and a drum was beating softly in a village somewhere where the rubber
    Negroes were going on with their slave lives.

THE SEA WIND

The sea wind sways on over the endless oceans —
spreads its wings night and day
rises and sinks again
over the desolate swaying floor of the immortal ocean.
Now it is nearly morning
or it is nearly evening
and the ocean wind feels in its face — the land wind.

Clockbuoys toll morning and evening psalms,
the smoke of a coalboat
or the smoke of a tar-burning Phoenician ship fades away at the
    horizons.
The lonely jellyfish who has no history rocks around with burning
    blue feet.
It's nearly evening now or morning.

DUSK IN THE COUNTRY

The riddle silently sees its image. It spins evening
among the motionless reeds.
There is a frailty no one notices
there, in the web of grass.

Silent cattle stare with green eyes.
They mosey in evening calm down to the water.
And the lake holds its immense spoon
up to all the mouths.

FROM HADES AND EUCLID
(*first version*)

1

When Euclid started out to measure Hades,
he found it had neither depth nor height.
Demons flatter than stingrays
swept above the plains of death,
their barks had no echoes as they ran
along the fire frontiers and the ice frontiers,
along the lines laid down in Hades.

Along the lines that fell apart
and joined again as lines
flock after flock of demons went abreast, in ranks, and parallel through
    Hades.

There were only waves, no hills, no chasms or valleys.
Only lines, parallel happenings, angles lying prone.
Demons shot along like elliptical plates;
they covered an endless field in Hades as though with moving
    dragonscales.

On the smoothed-over burial mounds that forgetfulness had destroyed
    with its flatness,
snakes were crawling—they were merely heavy lines:
lashed, crawled, stung their way
along the flowing lines.

A raging grassfire in roaring flatflight
rushed over the round like a carpenter's plane of fire.
It shot over the evil prairies, over the evil steppes, over the flat evil
    pusta
back and forth, ignited again and again by heat
on the flat fields in Hades.

2
The ovens of Hell lay close to the ground
on the flat fields.
There the capriciously damned were burned
in the brick rooms —
near the surface as graves are —
victims of flat evil,
with no comfort from a high place
or support from a low place,
received without dignity,
received without a rising,
received without any of the standards of eternity.
Their cries are met only by mockery
on the flat fields of evil.

And Euclid, the king of measurement, cried
and his cry went looking for Kronus, the god of spheres.

HENHOUSE

The hens drift in early from the day's pecking.
They take a few turns about the henhouse floor
and arrange themselves according to who's the favorite.
Then, when all that is clear,
the leaping up to the roost begins.
Soon they're all sitting in rows and the rooster is present.
He tests out sleep
but there is to be no sleep right away.
The hens shove to the side and cause trouble.
He has to straighten them out, with his beak and a cawkle.
Now it's shifting and settling down.
One of the hens tries to remember the last worm
she caught today.
But the memory is already gone down,
on its way through the crop.
Another hen, just before she falls asleep, recalls
the way the rooster looked, the white of her eyeballs fluttering,
her shutterlike lids closing out the world.

CÉSAR VALLEJO

THIS MAN IS so far out that he is only an inch away from his own face. Some poets may say that they don't feel well. Vallejo tells you that he is afraid that he is really an animal made of white snow. He creates in his poems paintings in words that suggest frightful things, and we do feel frightened, and wonder why the rest of the painters are painting flowers.

When I asked Neruda once about Vallejo, whom he knew well, he said that Vallejo was Peruvian, while he was merely Castillian: he implied that he saw things straight on, but Vallejo took things in from the side, in an Indian way. Vallejo, he said, has "a subtle way of thought, a way of expression that is not direct but oblique. I don't have it."

César Vallejo is not a poet of the partially authentic feeling, but a poet of the absolutely authentic. He does not hide part of his life, and describe only the more "poetic" parts. He lived a difficult life, full of fight, and in describing it never panders to a love of pleasantries nor a love of vulgarity. He had a tremendous feeling for, and love of, his family—his father, his mother, and his brothers—which he expresses with simple images of great resonance. His wildness and savagery exist side by side with a tenderness. The wildness and savagery rest on a clear compassion for others, and a clear intuition into his own inward path. He sees roads inside himself. In the remarkable intensity with which he follows a thought or an image, there is a kind of heroism. He follows the poem wherever it goes, even into the sea.

Vallejo's art is not in recapturing ideas but in actually thinking. We feel the flow of thought, its power like an underground river finding its way for the first time through some shifted ground — even he doesn't know where it will come out.

César Vallejo embodies the history of mankind, as Jung and Freud do, not by sprinkling the dust of the past on his words, but by thinking his way backward and forward through it.

He loves thinkers and refers to Marx, Feuerbach, Freud, Socrates, Aristotle again and again. At the same time he respects human suffering so much he is afraid all thought might be beside the point.

In *Poemas Humanas* especially, Vallejo suggests so well the incredible weight of daily life, how it pulls men and women down; carrying a day is like carrying a mountain. And what the weight of daily life wants to pull us down to is mediocrity. He hates it. Vallejo wants life and literature to be intense or not at all.

> And what if after so many wings of birds
> the stopped bird doesn't survive!
> It would be better then, really,
> if it were all swallowed up, and let's end it!

It is this marvelous intensity that is his mark. We all know poets who are able to make quick associations when there are not many mammal emotions around, but when anger or anguish enters the poem, they become tongue-tied, or lapse into clichés. Vallejo does just the opposite. Under the pressure of powerful human feeling, he leaps about wildly, each leap throwing him further out onto the edges of consciousness, and at the same time deeper into the "depths."

CÉSAR VALLEJO was born March 15, 1892, in a small mining town, Santiago de Chuco, in northern Peru; his family were Indians. The Indians worked on haciendas with little pay, and terrible housing. His brother worked in the office of a tungsten mine. Vallejo's father was governor of the town; César had eight brothers and sisters. He received a bachelor's degree at the University of Trujillo in 1916, and belonged to a lively group of students and writers who wanted revolution. They read Ruben Dario, Walt Whitman, and many French poets. César became a schoolmaster, and apparently a good one. Some of his early poems written during this period were later collected in *Los Heraldos Negros*.

Vallejo moved to Lima, and there joined an active group of bohemian writers. When he returned one day to his hometown for a visit, a political quarrel broke out and a friend was killed by the police; Vallejo was put in jail for three months. There he wrote some of the poems that would appear in *Trilce*.

In 1923, he left South America for Paris, but his life there became a disaster. He slept at times in parks or the Paris Metro; he lived without warm clothes, and sometimes ate only potatoes. He often had no food at all. He developed elaborate theories such as how to step out of the Metro without wearing out your shoes, how to cross your legs without wearing out your trousers. One French woman from across the courtyard saw him sitting in a chair for thirty-six hours without moving; she went over to him. In January of 1929, they were married. The couple moved to Spain, and Vallejo wrote stories for Madrid newspapers. On their return to France, they were arrested and expelled for radical activity. Back in Spain, he met García Lorca, Alberti, and Salinas. It was there his book *Trilce* was published. In 1932, the couple were given permission to return to Paris. But he wrote few poems, and it was a time of great poverty again.

He went to Spain once more in 1937, for a congress of revolutionary writers. The Spanish Civil War spurred him to write poems once more. The poems were collected as *Poemas Humanas*. In the early months of 1938, he became sick, lived with a high fever for months, and died on April 15 on a rainy day.

THE BLACK RIDERS

There are blows in life so violent—don't ask me!
Blows as if from the hatred of God; as if before them,
the deep waters of everything lived through
were backed up in the soul. . . . Don't ask me!

Not many; but they exist. . . . They open dark ravines
in the most ferocious face and in the most bull-like back.
Perhaps they are the horses of that heathen Attila,
or the black riders sent to us by Death.

They are slips backward made by the Christs of the soul,
away from some holy faith that is sneered at by Events.
These blows that are bloody are the crackling sounds
from some bread that burns at the oven door.

And man . . . poor man! . . . poor man! He swings his eyes, as
when a man behind us calls us by clapping his hands;
swings his crazy eyes, and everything alive
is backed up, like a pool of guilt, in that glance.

There are blows in life so violent. . . . Don't ask me!

THE SPIDER

It is a huge spider, which can no longer move;
a spider which is colorless, whose body,
a head and an abdomen, is bleeding.

Today I watched it with great care. With what tremendous energy
to every side
it was stretching out its many feet.
And I have been thinking of its invisible eyes,
the death-bringing pilots of the spider.

It is a spider which was shivering, fixed
on the sharp ridge of a stone;
the abdomen on one side,
and on the other, the head.

With so many feet, the poor thing, and still it cannot
solve it! And seeing it
confused in such great danger,
what a strange pain that traveler has given me today!

It is a huge spider, whose abdomen
prevents him from following his head.
And I have been thinking of his eyes
and of his many, many feet . . .
And what a strange pain that traveler has given me!

GOD

I feel that God is traveling
so much in me, with the dusk and the sea.
With him we go along together. It is getting dark.
With him we get dark. All orphans . . .

But I feel God. And it seems
that he sets aside some good color for me.
He is kind and sad, like those who care for the sick;
he whispers with sweet contempt like a lover's:
his heart must give him great pain.

Oh, my God, I've only just come to you,
today I love so much in this twilight; today
that in the false balance of some breasts
I weigh and weep for a frail Creation.

And you, what do you weep for . . . you, in love
with such an immense and whirling breast. . . .
I consecrate you, God, because you love so much;
because you never smile; because your heart
must all the time give you great pain.

THE MULE DRIVERS

Mule driver, you walk along fantastically glazed with sweat.
The Menocucho ranch charges
daily one thousand troubles for life.
Twelve noon. We've arrived at the waist of the day.
The sun that hurts so much.

Mule driver, you gradually vanish with your red poncho,
enjoying the Peruvian folk song of your coca leaves.
And I, from a hammock,
from a century of irresolution,
brood over your horizon, mourned for
by mosquitoes, and by the delicate
and feeble song of a paca-paca bird.
In the end you'll arrive where you are supposed to arrive,
mule driver, behind your saintly burro, going
away . . .
away . . .

You are lucky then, in this heat in which
all our desires and all our intentions rear up;
when the spirit that hardly rouses the body
walks without coca, and does not succeed in pulling
its brute toward the western
Andes of Eternity.

THE RIGHT MEANING

"Mother, you know there is a place somewhere called Paris. It's a huge place and a long way off and it really is huge."

My mother turns up my coat collar, not because it's starting to snow, but in order that it may start.

My father's wife is in love with me, walking up, always keeping her back to my birth, and her face toward my death. Because I am hers twice: by my good-bye and by my coming home. When I return home, I close her. That is why her eyes gave me so much, pronounced innocent of me, caught in the act of me, everything occurs through finished arrangements, through covenants carried out.

Has my mother confessed me, has she been named publicly? Why doesn't she give so much to my other brothers? To Victor, for example, the oldest, who is so old now that people say, "He looks like his father's youngest brother!" It must be because I have traveled so much! It must be because I have lived more!

My mother gives me illuminated permissions to explore my coming-home tales. Face-to-face with my returning-home life, remembering that I journeyed for two whole hearts through her womb, she blushes and goes deathly pale when I say in the discourse of the soul: "That night I was happy!" But she grows more sad, she grew more sad.

"How old you're getting, son!"

And she walks firmly through the color yellow to cry, because I seem to her to be getting old, on the blade of the sword, in the delta of my face. Weeps with me, grows sad with me. Why should my youth be necessary, if I will always be her son? Why do mothers feel pain when their sons get old, if their age will never equal anyway the age of the mothers? And why, if the sons, the more they get on, merely come nearer to the age of the fathers? My mother cries because I am old in my time and because I will never get old enough to be old in hers!

My good-byes left from a point in her being more toward the out-
side than the point in her being to which I come back. I am, because I
am so overdue coming back, more the man to my mother than the son
to my mother. The purity that lights us both now with three flames
lies precisely in that. I say then until I finally fall silent:

"Mother, you know there's a place somewhere called Paris. It's a
huge place and a long way off and it really is huge."

The wife of my father, hearing my voice, goes on eating her lunch,
and her eyes that will die descend gently along my arms.

I AM GOING TO TALK ABOUT HOPE

I do not feel this suffering as César Vallejo. I am not suffering now as a creative person, nor as a man, nor even as a simple living being. I don't feel this pain as a Catholic, or as a Mohammedan, or as an atheist. Today I am simply in pain. If my name weren't César Vallejo, I'd still feel it. If I weren't an artist, I'd still feel it. If I weren't a man, or even a living being, I'd still feel it. If I weren't a Catholic, or an atheist, or a Mohammedan, I'd still feel it. Today I am in pain from further down. Today I am simply in pain.

The pain I have has no explanations. My pain is so deep that it never had a cause, and has no need of a cause. What could its cause have been? Where is that thing so important that it stopped being its cause? Its cause is nothing, and nothing could have stopped being its cause. Why has this pain been born all on its own? My pain comes from the north wind and from the south wind, like those hermaphrodite eggs that some rare birds lay conceived of the wind. If my bride were dead, my suffering would still be the same. If they had slashed my throat all the way through, my suffering would still be the same. If life, in other words, were different, my suffering would still be the same. Today I am in pain from higher up. Today I am simply in pain.

I look at the hungry man's pain, and I see that his hunger walks somewhere so far from my pain that if I fasted until death, one blade of grass at least would always sprout from my grave. And the same with the lover! His blood is too fertile for mine, which has no source and no one to drink it.

I always believed up till now that all things in the world had to be either fathers or sons. But here is my pain that has neither a father nor a son. It hasn't any back to get dark, and it has too bold a front for dawning, and if they put it into some dark room, it wouldn't give light, and if they put it into some brightly lit room, it wouldn't cast a shadow. Today I am in pain, no matter what happens. Today I am simply in pain.

POEM TO BE READ AND SUNG

    I know there is someone
looking for me day and night inside her hand,
and coming upon me, each moment, in her shoes.
Doesn't she know the night is buried
with spurs behind the kitchen?

    I know there is someone composed of my pieces,
whom I complete when my waist
goes galloping on her precise little stone.
Doesn't she know that money once out for her likeness
never returns to her trunk?

    I know the day,
but the sun has escaped from me;
I know the universal act she performed in her bed
with some other woman's bravery and warm water, whose
shallow recurrence is a mine.
Is it possible this being is so small
even her own feet walk on her that way?

    A cat is the border between us two,
right there beside her bowl of water.
I see her on the corners, her dress — once
an inquiring palm tree — opens and closes. . . .
What can she do but change her style of weeping?

But she does look and look for me. This is a real story!

Translated by Robert Bly and James Wright

BLACK STONE LYING ON A WHITE STONE

I will die in Paris, on a rainy day,
on some day I can already remember.
I will die in Paris — and I don't step aside —
perhaps on a Thursday, as today is Thursday, in autumn.

It will be a Thursday, because today, Thursday, setting down
these lines, I have put my upper arm bones on
wrong, and never so much as today have I found myself
with all the road ahead of me, alone.

César Vallejo is dead. Everyone beat him,
although he never does anything to them;
they beat him hard with a stick and hard also

with a rope. These are the witnesses:
the Thursdays, and the bones of my arms,
the solitude, and the rain, and the roads . . .

Translated by Robert Bly and John Knoepfle

THE ROLL CALL OF BONES

They demanded in loud voices:
"We want him to show both hands at the same time."
And that simply couldn't be done.
"We want them to check the length of his steps while he cries."
And that simply couldn't be done.
"We want him to think one identical thought during the time a zero
    goes on being useless."
And that simply couldn't be done.
"We want him to do something crazy."
And that simply couldn't be done.
"We want a mass of men like him to stand in between him and another
    man just like him."
And that simply couldn't be done.
"We want him to compare him with himself."
And that simply couldn't be done.
"We want them to call him finally by his own name."
And that simply couldn't be done.

IN THE MOMENT

    In the moment the tennis player majestically launches
his ball, he possesses the rare innocence of an animal;
in the moment
the philosopher catches a new truth by surprise
he is a beast through and through.
Anatole France is very clear
that the religious impulse is produced by a bodily organ totally dedicated
and never before noticed,
in fact, we can go farther and state categorically
that in the very instant in which this organ is working at full power,
the man of faith is so empty of malice
as to be virtually a rutabaga.
Oh soul! Oh thought! Oh Marx! Oh Feuerbach!

I HAVE A TERRIBLE FEAR

I have a terrible fear of being an animal
of white snow, who has kept his father and mother
alive with his solitary circulation through the veins,
and a fear that on this day which is so marvellous, sunny,
     archbishoprical,
(a day that stands so for night)
this animal, like a straight line,
will manage not to be happy, or to breathe,
or to turn into something else, or to get money.

It would be a terrible thing
if I were a lot of man up to that point.
Unthinkable nonsense . . . an overfertile assumption
to whose accidental yoke the spiritual
hinge in my waist succumbs.
Unthinkable . . . Meanwhile
that's how it is on this side of God's head,
in the tabula of Locke, and of Bacon, in the pale neck
of the beast, in the snout of the soul.

And, in fragrant logic,
I do have that practical fear, this marvellous
moony day, of being that one, this one maybe,
to whose nose the ground smells like a corpse,
the unthinkable alive and the unthinkable dead.

306 | CÉSAR VALLEJO

Oh to roll on the ground, to be there, to cough, to wrap oneself,
to wrap the doctrine, the temple, from shoulder to shoulder,
to go away, to cry, to let it go for eight
or for seven or for six, for five, or let it go
for life with its three possibilities!

AND WHAT IF AFTER

And what if after so many words,
the word itself doesn't survive!
And what if after so many wings of birds
the stopped bird doesn't survive!
It would be better then, really,
if it were all swallowed up, and let's end it!

To have been born only to live off our own death!
To raise ourselves from the heavens toward the earth
carried up by our own bad luck,
always watching for the moment to put out our darkness with our
    shadow!
It would be better, frankly,
if it were all swallowed up, and the hell with it!

And what if after so much history, we succumb,
not to eternity,
but to these simple things, like being
at home, or starting to brood!
What if we discover later
all of a sudden, that we are living
to judge by the height of the stars
off a comb and off stains on a handkerchief!
It would be better, really,
if it were all swallowed up, right now!

They'll say we have a lot
of grief in one eye, and a lot of grief
in the other also, and when they look
a lot of grief in both. . . .
So then! . . . Naturally! . . . So! . . . Don't say a word!

THE ANGER THAT BREAKS A MAN DOWN INTO BOYS

The anger that breaks a man down into boys,
that breaks the boy down into equal birds,
and the bird, then, into tiny eggs;
the anger of the poor
owns one smooth oil against two vinegars.

The anger that breaks the tree down into leaves,
and the leaf down into different-sized buds,
and the buds into infinitely fine grooves;
the anger of the poor
owns two rivers against a number of seas.

The anger that breaks the good down into doubts,
and doubt down into three matching arcs,
and the arc, then, into unimaginable tombs;
the anger of the poor
owns one piece of steel against two daggers.

The anger that breaks the soul down into bodies,
the body down into different organs,
and the organ into reverberating octaves of thought;
the anger of the poor
owns one deep fire against two craters.

MASSES

When the battle was over,
and the fighter was dead, a man came toward him
and said to him: "Do not die; I love you so!"
But the corpse, it was sad! went on dying.

And two came near, and told him again and again:
"Do not leave us! Courage! Return to life!"
But the corpse, it was sad! went on dying.

Twenty arrived, a hundred, a thousand, five hundred thousand,
shouting: "So much love, and it can do nothing against death!"
But the corpse, it was sad! went on dying.

Millions of persons stood around him,
all speaking the same thing: "Stay here, brother!"
But the corpse, it was sad! went on dying.

Then all the men on the earth
stood around him; the corpse looked at them sadly, deeply moved;
he sat up slowly,
put his arms around the first man; started to walk . . .

NOVEMBER 10, 1937

MIGUEL HERNANDEZ

MIGUEL HERNANDEZ WAS a fierce fighter in words. He was born in the province of Alicante, and he wrote his first poems in the Gongora style of elaborate images, a practice in which the poet keeps from the reader the secret of what the poem is actually about. Here is a sample:

> For pulling the feathers from icy archangels,
> the lilylike snowstorm of slender teeth
> is condemned to the weeping of the fountains
> and the desolation of the running springs.

He published his first book, *Perito en Lunes* (*Expert in Moons*) in 1933 and sent copies to all the major poets of the day. When he gave readings, audiences could not solve the riddles. It took years before critics realized his "white narcissus" poem was not about the moon but a poem on shaving.

In April of 1933, he wrote to Federico García Lorca, whom he had met in Madrid, and complained. Lorca in his reply told him not to despair about the silence surrounding his first book.

> Your book stands deep in silence, like all first books, like my first, which had so much delight and strength. Write, read, study, and FIGHT! Don't be vain about your work. Your book is strong, it has many interesting things, and to eyes that can see makes clear *the passion of man,* but it doesn't, as you say, have more *cojones* than

those of the most established poets. Take it easy. Europe's most beautiful poetry is being written in Spain today. . . . Books of poetry, my dear Miguel, catch on very slowly.

I know perfectly well what you are like, and I send you my embrace like a brother, full of affection and friendship. (Write to me.) — Federico

Lorca returned to Madrid in 1934, and this time he met Neruda, who was a consul from Chile to Spain. Hernandez was tired of his own precious style, and in a famous review that he wrote of Neruda's *Residencia en la Tierra*, he said:

> I am sick of so much pure and minor art. I like the disordered and chaotic confusion of the Bible, where I see spectacular events, disasters, misfortunes, worlds turned over, and I hear outcries and explosions of blood.
>
> *(translated by Timothy Baland)*

Neruda mentioned that Miguel had a face like "a potato just lifted from the earth." He remembered Miguel's occasional visits to his house, his face and body still shining from his swim in the river.

On July 18, 1936, the Spanish Civil War officially began. On August 19, the Francoists killed Lorca. In September, Hernandez joined the Republican army. There's a photograph of him passionately reading to men with helmets on. His poems have changed:

> Today I am, I don't know how,
> today all I am ready for is suffering,
> today I have no friends,
> today the only thing I have is the desire
> to rip out my heart by the roots
> and stick it underneath a shoe

Today my destiny is too much for me.
And I'm looking for death down by my hands,
looking at knives with affection,
and I remember that friendly ax,
and all I think about is the tallest steeples
and making a fatal leap serenely.

The passage above is from some uncollected poems written by Hernandez in 1936. The rest of his life, he was deeply connected to the war, and he died in a Franco prison.

MIGUEL HERNANDEZ was born on October 30, 1910, in the village of Orihuela in Alicante Province. The family were goatherders. He had somewhere between two and seven years of school. In 1916, Miguel had to leave school at his father's insistence and join his brother and father herding goats and sheep.

The Canon of the cathedral at Orihuela took an interest in Hernandez and gave him the old classical Spanish literature of Cervantes, Lope de Vega, St. John of the Cross, and Frey Luis de Leon. Miguel especially loved the elaborate Gongora style and he wrote beautifully incomprehensible poems in this style. He met two poets of the neighborhood, Manon and Gabriel Sijé. They helped Miguel with early publications, but Miguel did not want to be typecast as a shepherd poet, and, against much advice, moved to Madrid in December of 1931 to get acquainted with the literary world. He met a few poets devoted to the Gongora style, but not much happened; after six months there, he returned to Orihuela.

Hernandez met and fell in love with Josefina Manresa, whose father belonged to the Guardia Civil. In 1934, he moved to Madrid again, but on a return visit to his hometown in January of 1936, he was arrested by the Guardia, beaten, and held in the barracks. Neruda, as the Chilean consul, arranged for Hernandez's release. A letter of protest against the arrest was signed by Lorca, Neruda, Alberti, and many others.

In August 1936, Manuel Manresa, the father of Josefina, was killed by leftists. In the same month, the Franco police shot García Lorca. After some months spent digging trenches around Madrid, he was sent to give readings to the men at the front and on radio stations.

In March of 1937, he and Josefina were married, and in June he helped organize the Second International Conference of Anti-Fascist Writers, attended by Auden, Neruda, Spender, Vallejo, and many others. In October, he was sent back to the front lines. On March 29, 1938, the war ended with the leftists defeated. Hernandez fled to Portugal, but was turned back at the border. There he was arrested by the Guardia Civil and beaten. He was held in Torrijos Prison in Madrid. Neruda worked furiously to get him released and a cardinal petitioned Franco for Hernandez's release. Against the warnings of friends, he returned to Orihuela, but two weeks later he was rearrested and taken to prison in Orihuela and then to a prison in Madrid. With twenty others, he was charged and sentenced to death. The government issued a flyer:

> Miguel Hernandez, condemned to death.
> Crime: Poet and soldier of the mother country.
> Aggravating, intelligentsia.
> Death to the intelligentsia.

His sentence was later commuted to thirty years in prison, but Hernandez died of tuberculosis on March 28, 1942.

YOU THREW ME A LEMON

You threw me a lemon, oh it was sour,
with a warm hand, that was so pure
it never damaged the lemon's architecture.
I tasted the sourness anyway.

With that yellow blow, my blood moved
from a gentle laziness into an anguished
fever, for my blood felt the bite
from a long and firm tip of a breast.

Yet glancing at you and seeing the smile
which that lemon-colored event drew from you,
so far from my dishonorable fierceness,

my blood went to sleep in my shirt,
and the soft and golden breast turned
to a baffling pain with a long beak.

FOR PULLING THE FEATHERS
FROM ICY ARCHANGELS

For pulling the feathers from icy archangels
the lilylike snowstorm of slender teeth
is condemned to the weeping of the fountains
and the desolation of the running springs.

For diffusing its soul into metals,
for abandoning the sunrises to the iron,
the stormy blacksmiths drag away the fire
to the anguish of the brutal anvils.

I see myself rushing recklessly toward the painful
retribution of the thorn, to the fatal
discouragement of the rose, and the aciduous

power of death, and so much ruin
is not for any sin or any other thing
except loving you, only for loving you.

YOUR HEART? — IT IS A FROZEN ORANGE

Your heart? — it is a frozen orange,
inside it has juniper oil but no light
and a porous look like gold: an outside
promising risks to the man who looks.

My heart is a fiery pomegranate,
its scarlets clustered, and its wax opened,
which could offer you its tender beads
with the stubbornness of a man in love.

Yes, what an experience of sorrow it is
to go to your heart and find a frost
made of primitive and terrifying snow!

A thirsty handkerchief flies through the air
along the shores of my weeping,
hoping that he can drink in my tears.

I HAVE PLENTY OF HEART

Today I am, I don't know how,
today all I am ready for is suffering,
today I have no friends,
today the only thing I have is the desire
to rip out my heart by the roots
and stick it underneath a shoe.

Today that dry thorn is growing strong again,
today is the day of crying in my kingdom,
depression unloads today in my chest
a depressed heavy metal.

Today my destiny is too much for me.
And I'm looking for death down by my hands,
looking at knives with affection,
and I remember that friendly ax,
and all I think about is the tallest steeples
and making a fatal leap serenely.

If it weren't for . . . I don't know what,
my heart would write a suicide note,
a note I carry hidden there,
I would make an inkwell out of my heart,
a fountain of syllables, and goodbyes and gifts,
and *you stay here* I'd say to the world.

I was born under a rotten star.
My grief is that I have only one grief
and it weighs more than all the joys together.

A love affair has left me with my arms hanging down
and I can't lift them anymore.
Don't you see how disillusioned my mouth is?
How unsatisfied my eyes are?

The more I look inward the more I mourn!
Cut off this pain? —who has the scissors?

Yesterday, tomorrow, today
suffering for everything,
my heart is a sad goldfish bowl,
a pen of dying nightingales.

I have plenty of heart.

Today to rip out my heart,
I who have a bigger heart than anyone,
and having that, I am the bitterest also.

I don't know why, I don't know how or why
I let my life keep on going every day.

SITTING ON TOP OF CORPSES

Sitting on top of corpses
fallen silent over the last two months,
I kiss empty shoes
and take hold wildly
of the heart's hand
and the soul that keeps it going.

I want my voice to climb mountains,
descend to earth, and give out thunder:
this is what my throat wants
from now on, and always has.

Come near to my loud voice,
nation of the same mother,
tree whose roots hold
me as in a jail.
I am here to love you,
I am here to fight for you,
with my mouth and blood
as with two faithful rifles.

If I came out of the dirt
and was born from a womb
with no luck and no money,
it was only that I might become
the nightingale of sadness,
an echo chamber for disaster,
that I could sing and keep singing
for the men who ought to hear it

everything that has to do with suffering,
with poverty, with earth.

Yesterday the people woke
naked, with nothing to pull on,
hungry, with nothing to eat,
and now another day has come
dangerous, as expected,
bloody, as expected.
In their hands, rifles
long to become lions
to finish off the animals
who have been so often animals.

Although you have so few weapons,
nation with a million strengths,
don't let your bones collapse:
as long as you have fists,
fingernails, spit, courage,
insides, guts, balls, and teeth,
attack those who would wound us.
Stiff as the stiff wind,
gentle as the gentle air,
kill those who kill,
loathe those who loathe
the peace inside you
and the womb of your women.
Don't let them stab you in the back;
live face-to-face and die
with your chest open to the bullets
and wide as the walls.

I sing with a griever's voice,
my people, for all your heroes,
your anxieties like mine,
your setbacks whose tears were drawn
from the same metal as mine,
suffering of the same mettle,
your thinking and my brain,
your courage and my blood,
your anguish and my honors,
all made of the same timber.
To me this life is like
a rampart in front of emptiness.

I am here in order to live
as long as my soul is alive,
and I am here to die
when that time comes,
deep in the roots of the nation,
as I will be and always have been.
Life is a lot of hard gulps,
but death is only one.

LETTER

The pigeon-house of letters
opens its impossible flight
from the trembling tables
on which memory leans,
the weight of absence,
the heart, the silence.

I hear the wingbeat of letters
sailing toward their center.
Wherever I go I meet
men and women badly
wounded by absence,
wasted by time.

Letters, descriptions, letters,
postcards, dreams,
bits of tenderness
planned in the sky,
sent from blood to blood,
from one longing to another.

Even though my loving body
lies under the earth now,
write to me here on earth
so I can write to you.

Old letters, old envelopes,
grow taciturn in the corner,
and the color of time pressed
down on the writing.

The letters slowly perish there
full of tiny shudders.
The ink feels death agony,
the loose sheets begin to fail,
and the paper fills with holes
like a diminutive cemetery
of emotions now gone,
of loves to come later.

Even though my loving body
lies under the earth now,
write to me here on earth
so I can write to you.

When I'm about to write you
even the inkwells get excited:
those black and frozen wells
blush and start quivering,
and a transparent human warmth
rises from the black deeps.
When I start to write you
my bones are ready to do it:
I write you with the permanent
ink of my love.

There goes my warm letter,
a dove forged in the fire,
its two wings folded down
and the address in the center.
A bird that only wants
your body, your hands, your eyes
and the space around your breath

for a nest of air and heaven.
And you will stay there naked
inside of your emotions,
without clothes, so you can feel
it wholly against your breast.

Even though my loving body
lies under the earth now,
write to me here on earth
so I can write to you.

Yesterday a letter was left
unclaimed, without an owner:
flying over the eyes
of someone who had lost his body.
Letters that stay alive
and talk for the dead:
wistful paper, human,
without eyes to look at it.

As the eyeteeth keep growing,
I feel the gentle voice
of your letter closer each time
like a great shout.
It will come to me asleep
if I can't manage to be awake.
And my wounds will become
the spilt inkwells,
the mouths that quiver,
remembering your kisses,
and they will repeat
in a voice no one has heard: I love you.

LULLABY OF THE ONION

*(Lines for his son, after receiving a letter from his wife in which
she said that all she had to eat was bread and onions.)*

An onion is frost
shut in and poor.
Frost of your days
and of my nights.
Hunger and onion,
black ice and frost
huge and round.

My son is lying now
in the cradle of hunger.
The blood of an onion
is what he lives on.
But it is your blood,
with sugar on it like frost,
onion and hunger.

A dark woman
turned into moonlight
pours herself down thread
by thread over your cradle.
My son, laugh,
because you can swallow the moon
when you want to.

Lark of my house,
laugh often.
Your laugh is in your eyes
the light of the world.
Laugh so much
that my soul, hearing you,
will beat wildly in space.

Your laugh unlocks doors for me,
it gives me wings.
It drives my solitudes off,
pulls away my jail.
Mouth that can fly,
heart that turns to
lightning on your lips.

Your laugh is the sword
that won all the wars,
it defeats the flowers
and the larks,
challenges the sun.
Future of my bones
and of my love.

The body with wings beating,
the eyelash so quick,
life is full of color
as it never was.
How many linnets
climb with wings beating
out of your body!

I woke up and was an adult:
don't wake up.
My mouth is sad:
you go on laughing.
In your cradle, forever,
defending your laughter
feather by feather.

Your being has a flying range
so high and so wide
that your body is a newly
born sky.
I wish I could climb
back to the starting point
of your travel!

You laugh, eight months old,
with five orange blossoms.
You have five tiny
ferocities.
You have five teeth
like five new
jasmine blossoms.

They will be the frontier
of kisses tomorrow,
when you feel your rows
of teeth are a weapon.
You will feel a flame
run along under your teeth
looking for the center.

My son, fly away, into the
two moons of the breast:
the breast, onion-
sad, but you, content.
Stay on your feet.
Stay ignorant of what's happening,
and what is going on.

RUMI

As American readers have learned recently, Rumi is astounding, fertile, abundant, almost more an excitable library of poetry than a person. In his poems, Rumi often adopts the transparent "you," using it so beautifully that each of us feels as if we too were being spoken to. Coleman Barks has echoed that tender "you" so brilliantly in his translations that we will never get over our gratitude to him.

His *Mathnawi* is as complicated as Shakespeare's works in its self-contradicting, high-spirited, chaotic, indulgent, loving, gossiping, outrageous, obscene, passionate, witty poetry, which is immensely learned. His poetry in its abundance seems to be a gift presented by half-mad lovers who have been doing the same work for hundreds of years.

When I started reading Rumi, all at once I felt at home. I think many readers of his work have that feeling. It's almost as if his poems resonate in some echo chamber that we retain only in memory. Some people say we once had that ecstatic love poetry in the religious culture around the Albigensians in southern France in the thirteenth and fourteenth centuries. The Albigensians brought to the troubadours the concept of *amor.* That teaching was hated by the more dogmatic and rigid fathers at Rome. In fact, one joke at that time, which was discussed in public meetings, was that *amor* is *roma* spelled backward. The Catholics held, for example, that real love was only possible inside marriage, the Albigensians that real love was only possible outside of marriage. All that ended when Simon de Montfort, supported by the Church, invaded southern France and destroyed the culture utterly.

Orthodox Islam, on its side, has always been uneasy as well about the ecstatic tradition of the Sufis and the lovers. The orthodox Muslims murdered several Sufis, among them Al-Hallaj, but they never undertook the wholesale murder of the ecstatic culture in the way the Christians did. Though often threatened, the Sufi culture survived in a number of Middle Eastern cities, among them Konya. It was there, with the help of Shams, that Rumi wrote the poems that still seem so amazing.

RUMI was born in what is now Afghanistan, in Balkh on September 30, 1204. His father was a well-known theologian. It is said that the Prophet gave him a special title in a dream which all the scholars in Balkh experienced on the same night. Balkh was at that time one of the centers of Islamic learning, as it had earlier been a center of Buddhism. Rumi inherited from his own father doubts about the dominant place of intellect in religion. Because the Mongols were approaching from the north, Rumi left with his family in 1218. It was a wise move. In 1220, thousands of people in Balkh were killed and the city entirely destroyed.

There's a story that in the travelings of Rumi's family, they visited the great poet Attar in Nishapur. Attar apparently sensed the genius of the young Rumi and gave him a copy of his book. Rumi's family then made a pilgrimage to Mecca, afterwards visiting Damascus. Finally, around 1125, they reached central Anatolia, in the area known as Rum. So "Rumi" means "from Rum."

Rumi's father was called to the city of Konya by Sultan Kaykobed, who gathered scholars and mystics from many countries. The father became an important teacher, and when he died in 1231, his son Jalaluddin was appointed to his place. A favorite discipline of Sufis was the chilla, that is, a period of solitude and prayer that lasts forty days. Jalaluddin apparently experienced a number of these chillas.

By 1242, the Mongol armies were coming close. The rulers of Konya paid heavy tributes to them and so the city was saved. In late October 1244, a strange event occurred. Shams, who was a wandering ascetic, stopped Rumi's donkey as Rumi was returning from a lecture, and threw him a difficult question about the difference between Mohammed and Bayazid. The two masters recognized the genius in each other, and Rumi decided to remain in seclusion with Shams for six months, abandoning his classes and family. The two of them talked "without eating, drinking or any human needs." When Shams disappeared, Rumi felt all the anguish of the abandoned lover. He had not paid much attention to Persian poetry and music, but he began now to write poems and sing them, as well as to dance. After a long search, Shams was finally located in Damascus, and Rumi brought him back to Konya, had him move in, and married him to one of Rumi's adopted daughters. The time of ecstasy between the two men resumed, but there was enormous jealousy. On December 5, 1248, when Rumi and Shams were talking late at night, someone knocked at the door. Shams went out and was killed, perhaps with the help of Rumi's second son, Alludin. No one was sure what had happened, and Rumi himself went out this time searching for Shams, but Shams was not found. Rumi wrote and named his collection of ecstatic poems *The Works of Shams of Tabriz*.

Rumi later became fond of several other confidants, to whom he dictated more poems, as well as the fables and jokes that make up the *Mathnawi*, which is an enormous work of more than 50,000 lines. Rumi died on December 17, 1273, at sunset. His tomb still stands in Konya, and hundreds visit it each day.

THE CAPTAIN WHO WALKS ON HIS DECK

The dictionaries have no entry for the sort of love we praise.
If you can define a road, it's not the Lover's road.
The high branches of love shoot into the air that existed before eternity.
And the roots grow down into the earth that exists after eternity.
This branch of love is beyond the divine throne and beyond the
    Pleiades.
We have pulled reason down from his throne.
We've broken up all the set rules for animal desire and instinctual life.
The kind of love that we know of is too great for sober reason
And too great for this simple instinctual life.
Now if you believe that your need can be met by something on the
    outside,
And your wanting satisfied from the outside,
You are really a tiger or a cougar.
Are you praying any longer to wooden idols? If not,
Then why do you keep praying to your desire?
If you become the one you long for, what will you do with your longing?
The Captain stalks on the deck of his ship. The planks are his fears
Of the bad things that may happen, and the joists
Are his longing for the marvellous things that may happen.
When the planks and the joists both go, nothing remains but the
    drowning.
Shams al Tabriz is the ocean, and also the pearl deep in the ocean.
His personality is the one secret the Holy One never gave away.

LOVE AND SILENCE

Love cuts a lot of arguments short.
It helps when you're with intellectuals.
The lover decides he won't say any more,
Afraid the pearl may fall out of his mouth.
As when Mohammed recited parts of the Koran,
Think how still and alert his companions became,
As when a bird lights on your head, and you barely breathe.
You don't cough or sneeze, lest it fly away.
If anyone speaks, whether sweet or sour, you say, "Shhh . . ."
Awe resembles the bird that makes you quiet.
Awe and wonder put a lid on the kettle as soon as your love inside is
    boiling.

EATING POETRY

My poems resemble the bread of Egypt—one night
Passes over the bread, and you can't eat it anymore.

So gobble my poems down now, while they're still fresh,
Before the dust of the world settles on them.

Where a poem belongs is here, in the warmth of the chest;
Out in the world it dies of cold.

You've seen a fish—put him on dry land,
He quivers for a few minutes, and then is still.

And even if you eat my poems while they're still fresh,
You still have to bring forward many images yourself.

Actually, friend, what you're eating is your own imagination.
These poems are not just some bare statements and old proverbs.

WALKING WITH OTHERS

It's important to join the crowds of those traveling.
You know, even Mohammed's horse ascended
In the throngs of meditators.
Such a lifting doesn't resemble a man rising to the moon,
It's more like grapes being lifted up into wine.
Mist rises when water boils, but that's not it. It's more like
An embryo changing into a person capable of thought.

THE EDGE OF THE ROOF

I don't like it here, I want to go back.
According to the old Knowers
If you're absent from the one you love
Even for one second that ruins the whole thing!

There must be someone . . . just to find
One *sign* of the other world in this town
Would be helpful.

You know the great Chinese Simurgh bird
Got caught in this net . . .
And what can I do? I'm only a wren.

My desire-body, don't come
Strolling over this way.
Sit where you are, that's a good place.

When you want dessert, you choose something rich.
In wine, you look for what is clear and firm.
What is the rest? The rest is mirages,
And blurry pictures, and milk mixed with water.
The rest is self-hatred, and mocking other people, and bombing.

So just be quiet and sit down.
The reason is: you are drunk,
And this is the edge of the roof.

TELL ME, WHAT HAVE I LOST?

I lived for thousands and thousands of years as a mineral and then I
   died and became a plant.
And I lived for thousands and thousands of years as a plant and then
   I died and became an animal.
And I lived for thousands and thousands of years as an animal and
   then I died and became a human being.
Tell me, what have I ever lost by dying?

ECSTATIC LOVE IS AN OCEAN

Ecstatic love is an ocean, and the Milky Way is a flake of foam
    floating on that ocean.
The stars wheel around the North Pole, and ecstatic love, running in
    a wheel, turns the stars.
If there were no ecstatic love, the whole world would stop.
Do you think that a piece of flint would change into a plant
    otherwise?
Grass agrees to die so that it can rise up and receive a little of the
    animal's enthusiasm.
And the animal soul, in turn, sacrifices itself. For what?
To help that wind, through one light waft
Of which Mary became with child. Without that wind,
All creatures on Earth would be stiff as a glacier,
Instead of being as they are,
Locustlike, searching night and day for green things, flying.
Every bit of dust climbs toward the Secret One like a sapling.
It climbs and says nothing; and that silence is a wild praise of the
    Secret One.

THAT JOURNEYS ARE GOOD

If a fir tree had a foot or two like a turtle, or a wing,
Do you think it would just wait for the saw to enter?

You know the sun journeys all night under the Earth;
If it didn't, how could it throw up its flood of light in the east?

And salt water climbs with such marvellous swiftness to the sky.
If it didn't, how would the cabbages be fed with the rain?

Have you thought of Joseph lately? Didn't he leave his father in tears,
    going?
Didn't he then learn how to understand dreams, and give away grain?

And you, if you can't leave your country, you could go into yourself,
And become a ruby mine, open to the gifts of the sun.

You could travel from your manhood into the inner man, or from
    your womanhood into the inner woman—
By a journey of that sort Earth became a place where you find gold.

So leave your complaints and self-pity and internalized death-energy.
Don't you realize how many fruits have already escaped out of
    sourness into sweetness?

A good source of sweetness is a teacher; mine is named Shams.
You know every fruit grows more handsome in the light of the sun.

PRAISING MANNERS

We should ask God
To help us toward manners. Inner gifts
Do not find their way
To creatures without just respect.

If a man or woman flails about, he not only
Smashes his house,
He burns the whole world down.

Your depression is connected to your insolence
And your refusal to praise. If a man or woman is
On the path, and refuses to praise—that man or woman
Steals from others every day—in fact is a shoplifter!

The sun became full of light when it got hold of itself.
Angels began shining when they achieved discipline.
The sun goes out whenever the cloud of not-praising comes near.
The moment that foolish angel felt insolent, he heard the door close.

THE DRUNKARDS

The drunkards are rolling in slowly, those who hold to wine are
    approaching.
The lovers come, singing, from the garden, the ones with brilliant
    eyes.

The I-don't-want-to-lives are leaving, and the I-want-to-lives are arriving.
They have gold sewn into their clothes, sewn in for those who have
    none.

Those with ribs showing who have been grazing in the old pasture
    of love
Are turning up fat and frisky.

The souls of pure teachers are arriving like rays of sunlight
From so far up to the ground-huggers.

How marvellous is that garden, where apples and pears, both for
    the sake of the two Marys,
Are arriving even in winter.

Those apples grow from the Gift, and they sink back into the Gift.
It must be that they are coming from the garden to the garden.

THE MILL, THE STONE,
AND THE WATER

All our desire is a grain of wheat.
Our whole personality is the milling-building.
But this mill grinds without knowing about it.

The mill stone is your heavy body.
What makes the stone turn is your thought-river.
The stone says: I don't know why we all do this, but the river has
    knowledge!

If you ask the river, it says,
I don't know why I flow.
All I know is that a human opened the gate!

And if you ask the person, he says:
All I know, oh gobbler of bread, is that if this stone
Stops going around, there'll be no bread for your bread-soup!

All this grinding goes on, and no one has any knowledge!
So just be quiet, and one day turn
To God, and say: "What is this about bread-making?"

THE HAWK

We are a little crazier now, and less sober, and some joy has risen out
 of us . . . it was so glad to be gone . . .

When it noticed the sober water no longer was holding its leg, it
 flew—

It is not in the mountains nor the marshes, it has sent itself to be with
 the Holy One who is alone.

Don't look here and there in the house, it belongs to air, it is made of
 air, and has gone into air.

This is a white hawk that belongs to Gawain's master; it belongs to
 him and has gone to him.

THE TWELVE LIES

People say, "The one you love is unfaithful."
That's the first lie.

They say, "Your night will never end in dawn."
Did you hear that lie?

They say, "Why give up sleep and die for love? Once in the grave,
All that is forgotten; it's over."
That's the third lie.

Some thinkers say, "Once you leave our time system,
The spirit stops moving; in fact, it goes backwards."
People love to tell lies!

Daydreamers with sluggish eyes say,
"Your poems and your teaching stories are nothing but daydreams."
I heard that lie.

People running around in the underbrush say,
"There's no path to the mountain and no mountain either."
That's the sixth lie!

They say, "The keeper of secrets never tells
A single secret except to an intermediary."
People love that lie.

They say, "If you're a worker, you'll never receive the key;
The master alone goes to heaven."
That's the eighth lie.

They go on: "If you have too much earth in your chart,
You'll never grasp what angels are."
Another lie!

They like to say, "You'll never get out of this nest
With your stubby love wings; you'll drop like a stone."
Did you hear that lie?

They maintain, "What human beings do is insignificant anyway.
Stones weigh more than our evil. God cares nothing about it."
That's a big lie.

So just keep silent, and if anyone says to you,
"No communion takes place without words," just say to him,
"I heard that lie."

TWO KINDS OF MIRACLES

Miracles secret and open flow from the teacher.
That's reasonable—it's not unusual at all.
And the tiniest of these miracles
Is this: Everyone near a saint gets drunk with God.

When a spiritual man lets the water hold up his feet
We are moved, because by ways we cannot see
The sight of that links
The soul back to the source of all lightness.

Of course a saint can move a mountain!
But who cares about that? How marvellous is the bread
Made without dough, the dishes of food
That are invisible, Mary's grapes that never saw the vine!

HORACE

HORACE IS A cagey bringer of bad news. The reader needs to gain an appreciation of his tartness. He refers again and again to death coming toward us, using images as flavorful as those of Trakl or Vallejo.

When he's lying on the grass, drinking some old wine, he doesn't feel we should just relax:

Why do the darkling pines and the white
Delicate poplars weave their shady
Branches together, and the excited water
Work to curl itself around us?

There's something ominous in the whole afternoon:

Bring some roses, already turning dark,
And cardamom and wines; being rich
And young, we have to trust the dark threads
Of the Three Sisters are still unbroken.

The English used him for years to educate young men toward an even temperament. But here we're not in a typical Oxford mood; we're really in the mood of some Russian story with Baba Yaga in it. The boat can sink. The ground can open up any second.

You'll soon lose your cunningly acquired
Strips of woods, the estate by the yellow
Tiber, the Roman house, its silver and gold,
To some miserable heir, and it's over.

He's alert to the way human beings keep animals about to be sacrificed
inside fences. How does the sky look to them? What is this huge force
that prepares them for sacrifice?

Whether we descend from the great houses,
Or drift unprotected under the naked
Sky, it's all one; we are sacrifices
To Death, not well known for compassion.

Someone or something is keeping us, as humans keep herds.

We are obliged and herded. The lot is
Inside the urn; the ball with our number
Will roll out. And what we'll get
Is an everlasting absence from home.

There are hundreds of ways to translate his disturbing, under-
stated, ominous poems; I prefer the way in which we can feel fear.

You know that what most disturbs the soul
Is not Dindymene, nor that one who lives
With the Great Snake, nor the half-
Mad dancers with their crying metals,

It is grim-faced anger.

We don't feel Marvell here nor Whittier nor Alexander Pope; it's more like Robinson Jeffers:

> The Noric swords
> Cannot dissolve it, nor the ship-
> Swallowing sea, nor greedy fire, nor
> God himself when he comes roaring down.

HORACE was born on December 8, 65 B.C. His father was a freed slave who worked as an auctioneer in Apulia, near the heel of Italy, in a town founded by ex-soldiers. His father took him to Rome in order to find a good education for his son. Horace studied Greek in Rome and then in Athens. He was in his early twenties when Julius Caesar was murdered, and Brutus recruited him as a young regiment officer. He fought in the battle at Philippi, where he felt he was fighting for the old liberty against the fascism of Julius Caesar. After Brutus was killed in battle, Horace decided to throw down his shield and run. Once back in Italy, he found that his father's house had been confiscated. Three years later, many soldiers, Horace among them, received amnesty, and he apparently took a job in a treasury records office. By then, he was publishing poems.

Virgil noticed the poet, and asked the cultural lord, Maecenas, to help him. Maecenas did. Horace received a small farm in the Sabine Hills, where he lived the rest of his life.

One could say that his greatest gift was as a musician; he was a genius in sound. He managed to break up old sound habits so that Latin words fit into the old Greek song patterns, particularly the Alcaic pattern, which fixed all the short and long syllables for its four-lined form. (Tomas Tranströmer as a young man adapted the same Alcaic form to Swedish.) We know that both Alcaeus and Sappho sang their poems to stringed instruments, but there is no evidence that Horace did that. His odes in the Alcaic meter were not well received, and for six years, he gave up writing these concentrated, emotional poems. But the emperor Augustus admired Horace, and enticed him back to the Greek form, this time to Sappho's meter, by commissioning a triumphal ode. Horace died when he was fifty-six years old in 8 B.C. He was buried on a hill along with other famous Roman writers near the grave of Maecenas.

THE ANGER POEM

About my angry lines, burn them, do
Whatever you wish, or dip them
In the Adriatic Ocean; do this, hear me,
Handsome mother of a still more handsome daughter.

You know that what most disturbs the soul
Is not Dindymene, nor that one who lives
With the Great Snake, nor the half-
Mad dancers with their crying metals,

It is grim-faced anger. The Noric swords
Cannot dissolve it, nor the ship-
Swallowing sea, nor greedy fire, nor
God himself when he comes roaring down. . . .

Prometheus did what he did, he added a bit
To us from seals and orioles, dropped
Those bits into our clay, and had no choice
But to put into us the lion's mad angers.

Anger is what broke Thyeste's life,
And many shining cities went down brick
By brick before anger, and aggressive
Battalions ran their ploughs in great

Delight over ground covering those walls.
Calm your mind. Heat tempted
Me in my sweet early days, and sent
Me deeply mad to one-sided poems. Now

I want to replace those sour lines with
Sweet lines; now, having sworn off harsh
Attacks, I want you to become
My friend, and give me back my heart.

Book 1, Number 16

BRING ROSES AND CARDAMOM

To keep the soul serene even when the way is
Arduous, and to remain moderately unmoved
When gifts roll in, well, that's my advice for you,
Friend Dellius, for you are mortal too.

Evenness is best, whether disasters make
Everything crooked, or whether you can
Enjoy sipping, while you lie on your back
In the grass, the host's hidden-away wine.

Why do the darkling pines and the white
Delicate poplars weave their shady
Branches together, and the excited water
Work to curl itself around us?

Bring some roses, already turning dark,
And cardamom and wines; being rich
And young, we have to trust the dark threads
Of the Three Sisters are still unbroken.

You'll soon lose your cunningly acquired
Strips of woods, the estate by the yellow
Tiber, the Roman house, its silver and gold,
To some miserable heir, and it's over.

Whether we descend from the great houses,
Or drift unprotected under the naked
Sky, it's all one; we are sacrifices
To Death, not well known for compassion.

We are obliged and herded. The lot is
Inside the urn; the ball with our number
Will roll out. And what we'll get
Is an everlasting absence from home.

Book 2, Number 3

POEM FOR ARTEMIS

Doorkeeper of mountains and oak groves,
You who, when girls call three
Times to you as they are about to
Give birth, slip them past death.

A great mountain pine shades my roof; I give
This tree to you, and joyfully each November
I'll pour blood from a young boar on its ground,
A boar just learning to thrust his tusks to the side.

Book 3, Number 22

GRIEVING TOO LONG

Clouds do not send their rain down endlessly
On the rough-whiskered fields, and obstinate
Gales do not work up the Caspian Sea
The whole winter, nor in Armenia, dear friend,

Do glaciers remain there inert month
After month, and those oak-forested headlands
Facing the Adriatic don't have winds
Stripping leaves from branches all winter.

But you still weepily carry on about
The initiate in love you lost; your moans do
Not end even when the Western Star rises,
Nor when the Morning Star hurries away at dawn.

And yet that old man Nestor, who had lived three
Lives, did not mourn his son forever;
When they lost Troilus the lovable, his
Phrygian sisters and parents did not go on

And on. So it's good to check your endless
Lamentations; instead, let's take note of the gains
That our Caesar, called the Augustus, has
Made in the world—some Turkish peaks

Are lower now, the Euphrates waters are
A bit more constrained, the Medes are part
Of the Empire these days, and the Scythians riding
Over the steppes are, in fact, no longer nomads.

Book 2, Number 9

LET'S DO THIS POEM

Being a big favorite of the Muses, I'll appeal to
The winds to carry my depression off
To the seas of Crete. Which bearded German king,
Looking up at the Great Bear, worries us, or what disaster

Threatens Tiridatias in Persia, it's all
One with me. Giver of new poems,
Lover of the clear springs, weave some
Ornate lines as a gift for Lucius.

If you don't come, none of my honoring
Will take hold. Let's do this in Alcaic meter,
With its sonorities; you and your sisters, do
Come, let's make this boy immortal.

Book 1, Number 26

GHALIB

GHALIB IS IMPISH, reckless, obsessed with titles and distinctions, roguish, a breaker of religious norms, a connoisseur of sorrow, and a genius. He knows all the old poems of love and says:

> While telling the story, if each eyelash does not drip with blood
> You're not telling a love story, but a tale made for the kids.

Delhi, in his time (the mid-nineteenth century), had a lively culture and a vigorous tradition of poetry recitals, or mushiras, sponsored by the Mughal emperor. Ghalib's poems veered away from the traditional poetics clichés of the time, and were thought to be difficult.

> I have to write what's difficult; otherwise it's difficult to write.

Ghalib was a Muslim, and yet the wine he drank was not symbolic:

> Just put a wineglass and some wine in front of me;
> Words will fall out of my mouth like apple blossoms.

Ghalib's lines, so elegant and sparse, stretch the muscles that we use for truth, muscles we rarely use:

> My destiny did not include reunion with my Friend.
> Even if I lived a hundred years this failure would be the same.

It is as though when Kabir writes a letter to God, God always answers. We could say that when Ghalib writes a letter to God, God doesn't answer. Ghalib says:

> When I look out, I see no hope for change.
> I don't see how anything in my life can end well.

Ghalib's tart, spicy declaration of defeated expectations ranges over many subjects:

> Heart-sorrow eventually kills us, but that's the way the heart is.
> If there were no love, life would have done the trick.

This shift from the buoyant confidence of Kabir, Rumi, and Mirabai to the disappointment of Ghalib: what could it mean? Perhaps the turn to failure is natural six centuries after Rumi and four centuries after Kabir. Perhaps spiritual achievement involves more difficulty now than it did in the thirteenth century, or perhaps this change in tone has nothing to do with history at all. Perhaps Ghalib writes only six letters a day to God, instead of forty; perhaps he's distracted from the Road by the very love affairs that are to him the essence of the Road. He is a truth-teller around losing the Road. Awareness of this change was my first surprise.

We might look at the amazing way that Ghalib's ghazals are put together. No clear thread unites all the couplets. For example, if we return to the poem mentioned above, "My Spiritual State," which begins:

> When I look out, I see no hope for change.
> I don't see how anything in my life can end well.

we see a statement of theme. But a fresh theme, a little explosion of humor and sadness, arrives in the next stanza:

Their funeral date is already decided, but still
People complain that they can't sleep.

The third couplet, or *sher,* embarks on a third theme:

When I was young, my love-disasters made me burst out laughing.
Now even funny things seem sober to me.

It slowly becomes clear that we are dealing with a way of adventuring one's way through a poem utterly distinct from our habit of textual consistency in theme. Most of the poems we know, whether written in English, French, German, or Hausa, tend to follow from an idea clearly announced at the start. "Something there is that doesn't love a wall." The poet then fulfills the theme, often brilliantly, by drawing on personal experience, and by offering anecdotes, dreams, other voices: "Good fences make good neighbors." By the end, the theme is fulfilled. The ghazal form does not do that. It invites the reader to discover the hidden center of the poem or the hidden thought that ties it all together, a hidden center unexpressed by the poet himself or herself. I find this delicious. Moreover, when we arrive at the final *sher,* where, according to our typical expectations, the poet should clinch his argument, Ghalib often does exactly the opposite. He confounds everyone by making a personal remark:

Your talk about spiritual matters is great, O Ghalib.
You could have been thought of as a sage if you didn't drink all the time.

GHALIB was born in Agra on December 27, 1797. His grandfather, who was Turkish, had come to India from Samarkand as a military mercenary, working for the governor of Punjab and other emperors. His two sons continued in this profession, which was a dangerous one. Ghalib's father died when he was four. His mother belonged to an affluent family in Agra, and Ghalib lived in that house with his maternal relatives. He began writing poems in Persian when he was nine; all his life he loved the Persian language best, but wrote hundreds of poems in Urdu as well. Ghalib was married at thirteen and, shortly after, moved to Delhi where he remained the rest of his life. Delhi was the capital of the Mughal Empire; the emperor, Bahadur Shah, was of course subordinate to the British at that time. Inside the palace, however, called the Red Fort, the emperor was the Majesty, the Shadow of God, the Refuge of the World. The emperor held elaborate poetry readings twice a month in the palace. Ghalib became immensely famous as a poet in Delhi, even though his poems were considered very difficult.

He led a rather rakish life. He had many debts with wine sellers. For making poetry and drinking wine, he best loved "cloudy days and moonlit nights." Late at night when he was writing, with the help of wine, he would tie a knot in his long sash each time he finished a stanza. Finally he would go to bed, and in the morning, as he untied each knot, he would recall the stanza and write it down. He got into a lot of trouble with the Islamic authorities, and was arrested for gambling as well. A pension had been awarded to Ghalib's father, and that pension came down to him; Ghalib spent much time over the years making sure this pension continued.

In 1857, all that period of poetry readings and social lightheartedness came crashing down. The Delhi revolt against the British started in May of 1857. The rebels invaded the city, killed many English soldiers and officials, and razed their houses. The English took up position outside the city and four months later recaptured it with great brutality. They retook the Red Fort, flattening houses in a wide area around it in order to have the space clear for cannon. They began hanging Indians suspected of treason and ultimately hanged over 20,000 people. At one point, Colonel Brown began to call in persons of importance and question them. Most arrived dressed very soberly.

Ghalib arrived wearing red and yellow clothes and a conical hat. Colonel Brown asked, "Are you a Muslim?" "I'm half a Muslim." "How can that be?" "I don't eat pork, but I do drink." Colonel Brown was apparently amazed at this sort of reply, and questioned him no further.

Ghalib remained inside his own house, living very cautiously: "Death is cheap," he said, "and food expensive." During this time, he was often ill, had severe depressions, and was eventually bedridden with sores and swelling all over his body. Many of his poems had been lost. The poetry readings and the "exciting life" ended, and he still had twelve more years to live. But everything had changed. Nonetheless he went on writing his poems and continued to become embroiled in literary controversies. Ghalib died in 1869 and was given an official Sunni burial. His wife died exactly a year later.

My last breath is ready to go, is leaving.
And now, friends, God, only God exists.

All of the following translations of Ghalib have been done with the generous collaboration of Sunil Dutta.

WHEN THE DAY COMES

One can sigh, but a lifetime is needed to finish it.
We'll die before we see the tangles in your hair loosened.

There are dangers in waves, in all those crocodiles with their
    jaws open.
The drop of water goes through many difficulties before it becomes
    a pearl.

Love requires waiting, but desire doesn't want to wait.
The heart has no patience; it would rather bleed to death.

I know you will respond when you understand the state of my soul,
But I'll probably become earth before all that is clear to you.

When the sun arrives the dew on the petal passes through existence.
I am also me until your kind eye catches sight of me.

How long is our life? How long does an eyelash flutter?
The warmth of a poetry gathering is like a single spark.

O Ghalib, the sorrows of existence, what can cure them but death?
There are so many colors in the candle flame, and then the day comes.

THE CLAY CUP

If King Jamshid's diamond cup breaks, that's it.
But my clay cup I can easily replace, so it's better.

The delight of giving is deeper when the gift hasn't been demanded.
I like the God-seeker who doesn't make a profession of begging.

When I see God, color comes into my cheeks.
God thinks — this is a bad mistake — that I'm in good shape.

When a drop falls in the river, it becomes the river.
When a deed is done well, it becomes the future.

I know that Heaven doesn't exist, but the idea
Is one of Ghalib's favorite fantasies.

LEFTOVERS IN THE CUP

For my weak heart this living in the sorrow house is more than
    enough.
The shortage of rose-colored wine is also more than enough.

I'm embarrassed, otherwise I'd tell the wine server
That even the leftovers in the cup are, for me, enough.

No arrow comes flying in; I am safe from hunters.
The comfort level I experience in this cage is more than enough.

I don't see why the so-called elite people are so proud
When the ropes of custom that tie them down are clear enough.

It's hard for me to distinguish sacrifice from hypocrisy,
When the greed for reward in pious actions is obvious enough.

Leave me alone at the Zam Zam Well; I won't circle the Kaaba.
The wine stains on my robe are already numerous enough.

If we can't resolve this, today will be like the Last Day.
She is not willing and my desire is more than strong enough.

The blood of my heart has not completely exited through my eyes.
O death, let me stay awhile, the work we have to do is abundant
    enough.

It's difficult to find a person who has no opinion about Ghalib.
He is a good poet, but the dark rumors about him are more than
    enough.

MY DESTINY

My destiny did not include reunion with my Friend.
Even if I lived a hundred years this failure would be the same.

Your promise determined my life; but it was not believable.
If I had believed it, I would have died of joy anyway.

What kind of friendship is this when friends give advice?
I wish they knew healing or simple, ordinary sympathy.

Heart-sorrow eventually kills us, but that's the way the heart is.
If there were no love, life would have done the trick.

This night of separation, whom can I tell about it?
I think death would be better, because at least it doesn't repeat.

Your hesitation indicates that the thread you had tied is weak;
You would never have broken the thread had it been strong.

Ask my heart sometime about your arrow shot from a loose bow.
It would not have hurt so much if it had actually gone through.

Rocks are hard, so they don't cry, but if your pain
Were genuine, Ghalib, it would make even rocks cry.

After my death, my reputation worsened. Maybe if I had just
    drowned
In a river, and had no tomb, they would have let Ghalib alone.

This great one, who can possibly see her? She is this One.
With just a hint of two, we might have achieved a meeting.

Your talk about spiritual matters is great, O Ghalib.
You could have been thought of as a sage if you didn't drink all
    the time.

QUESTIONS

Since nothing actually exists except You,
Then why do I keep hearing all this noise?

These magnificent women with their beauty astound me.
Their side glances, their eyebrows, how does all that work? What is it?

These palm trees and these tulips, where did they come from?
What purpose do they serve? What are clouds and wind?

We hope for faithfulness and loyalty from people.
But people don't have the faintest idea what loyalty is.

Good rises from good actions, and that is good.
Beyond that, what else do saints and good people say?

I am willing to give up my breath and my life for You,
Even though I don't know the first thing about sacrifice.

The abundant objects of the world mean nothing at all!
But if the wine is free, how could Ghalib hang back?

DON'T SKIMP WITH ME TODAY

For tomorrow's sake, don't skimp with me on wine today.
A stingy portion implies a suspicion of heaven's abundance.

The horse of life is galloping; we'll never know the stopping place.
Our hands are not touching the reins nor our feet the stirrups.

I keep a certain distance from the reality of things.
It's the same distance between me and utter confusion.

The scene, the one looking and the ability to see are all the same.
If that is so, why am I confused about what is in front of me?

The greatness of a river depends on what it shows to us.
If we separate it into bubbles and waves, we are lost.

She is not free from her ways to increase her beauty.
The mirror she sees is on the inside of her veil.

What we think is obvious is so far beyond our comprehension.
We are still dreaming even when we dream we are awake.

From the smell of my friend's friend I get the smell of my friend.
Listen, Ghalib, you are busy worshiping God's friend.

MY SPIRITUAL STATE

When I look out, I see no hope for change.
I don't see how anything in my life can end well.

Their funeral date is already decided, but still
People complain that they can't sleep.

When I was young, my love disasters made me burst out laughing.
Now even funny things seem sober to me.

I know the answer—that's what keeps me quiet.
Beyond that it's clear I know how to speak.

Why shouldn't I scream? I can stop. Perhaps
The Great One notices Ghalib only when he stops screaming.

This is the spiritual state I am in:
About myself, there isn't any news.

I do die; the longing for death is so strong it's killing me.
Such a death comes, but the other death doesn't come.

What face will you wear when you visit the Kaaba?
Ghalib, you are shameless even to think of that.

MY HEAD AND MY KNEES

If I didn't cry all the time, my house would still be desolate.
The ocean is huge and empty, just like the desert.

Am I to complain about the narrowness of my heart?
It's unbelieving; no matter what happened, it would have been confused.

If I were patient for a lifetime, the Doorkeeper would surely let me in.
The doorkeeper of your house could model itself on such a heart.

Before anything, there was God; had there been nothing, there would
    have been God.
It was because I lived that I died. If I had never lived, what would
    have become of me?

Sorrow stunned my head; so why should I feel bad about my beheading?
If it hadn't been detached, it would be resting on my knees anyway.

Ghalib died centuries ago. But we still remember his little questions:
"What is before God?" "If I had never been born, how would that be?"

SOME EXAGGERATIONS

The world I see looks to me like a game of children.
Strange performances and plays go on night and day.

King Solomon's throne is not a big thing to me.
I hear Jesus performed miracles, but I'm not interested.

The idea that the world exists is not acceptable to me.
Illusion is real, but not the things of the world.

The desert covers its head with sand when I appear with my troubles.
The river rubs its forehead in the mud when it sees me.

Don't ask me how I am when I am parted from you.
I notice that your face turns a little pale when you're near me.

People are right to say that I love looking at myself, but sitting
In front of me is a beauty whose face is bright as a mirror.

Just put a wineglass and some wine in front of me;
Words will fall out of my mouth like apple blossoms.

People imagine that I hate, but it's merely jealousy.
That's why I scream: "Don't say her name in my presence!"

Faith pulls me in one direction, but disbelief pulls me in another.
The Kaaba stands far behind me, and the Church stands next to me.

I am a lover; therefore, charming a woman is my work.
When she is near me, Laila makes fun of Majnoon.

The time of reunion brings happiness rather than death.
When reunion came, I remembered the night of parting.

We have a sea of blood now with large waves.
I am content with it; I know worse could happen.

My hands move with difficulty, but at least my eyes are lively.
Just leave the glass and the wine jug standing where they are.

Ghalib is a Muslim also, so we know a lot of each other's secrets.
Please don't speak badly of Ghalib when I'm around.

HAFEZ

As WE READ a Hafez poem, we are tasting some sweetness that has been preserved by lovers and poets for a thousand years. Hafez's poetry is so amazing that some Persians consider it another thing entirely—something more complicated than poetry. He achieves drunkenness through sobriety, and a wildness through perfect form. Hafez often stretches his poem far back into time, into "Pre-Eternity."

I have dropped in a heap on the earth, crying,
In the hope that I will feel a touch of His hand . . .

How blessed is the man who, like Hafez,
Has tasted in his heart the wine made before Adam.

A poem of Hafez's moves steadily forward, somewhat like a Bach prelude; it reaches into the invisible world with its first note, and the low notes bring up the endless sorrow of life on earth. The left hand goes on talking of failure and repentance, and the light, quick right hand talks about the magnificence of poetry and religion, of the side glances given to us by God. Both hands together move toward a perfection that belongs more to angels than to human beings.

Your perch is on the lote tree in Paradise,
Oh wide-seeing hawk. What are you doing
Crouching in this mop closet of calamity?

Hafez wrote about 480 ghazals. Inside them, he sometimes converses with other poets of his time, embedding phrases from another person's poem. In that way he honors other poets, and the poets could be said to be working on some huge poem together. It is as if Blake had found a community of forty other poets in England, who also worked on the poems of Eternity. Such was the immense spiritual culture of Persia in the fourteenth century.

Anne Marie Schimmel mentions that we can feel in each stanza of Hafez the smoke of this world and the clarity of the spiritual world. He is fond of the resources of the Islamic creation myth. A Hafez stanza may contain one elaborate Islamic doctrine after another, summed up swiftly like crystals formed under great pressure. He adopts the metaphors of the old Zoroastrian religion:

> Last night I heard angels pounding on the door
> Of the tavern. They had been kneading clay and they
> Threw the clay of Adam in the shape of a wine cup.

Priests of the Zoroastrian religion sold wine at the temple, and so the words *tavern* and *wine* in his work delicately refer to the esoteric religion of love that we know in Western culture from the troubadours. He won't accept the fear of women that is such a striking tone of the Islamic mullahs. He reports in one poem that a "wild daughter has shown up missing."

> Reason is lost with her . . . beware, your sleep may not be safe.
> She is a night-woman of sharp taste, delicate, rosy . . .
> If you should happen to find her, please bring her to Hafez's house.

HAFEZ was born in Shiraz, southwest of Tehran, probably in A.D. 1320 (the year before Dante died). His father, who was a coal merchant, read the Koran to him, and the boy began to memorize it and many poems of earlier poets as well. His pen name was Hafez, which means someone who has memorized the Koran. He had to leave school in order to help support the family, working in a drapery shop and a bakery. He probably worked as a copyist too. The library in Tashkent has a copy of Amir Khusrau's *Kamsa* in Hafez's hand, dated February 9, 1355. He learned mathematics and astronomy, as well as Arabic and Turkish.

The story goes that one day he fell in love with the daughter of a wealthy man when delivering bread to their house. It wasn't a successful courtship, but he began to write poems at this time. Eventually his poetry became very famous. Several kings, including the emperor of the Bahmanid kingdom in south India, invited him to live there, but he accepted none of the invitations. We do know that he was married, that he had children; he wrote an elegy for his son who died in 1362.

During his lifetime, Tamburlane's invasion from the north was proceeding. He reached Shiraz in 1387, the same year in which he and his army massacred 70,000 people in Isfahan. Tamburlane stayed for two months in Shiraz. A well-known stanza of Hafez went:

For the Hindu mole of that Shirazy Turk who attracts
Our hearts, I would give all of Samarkand and Bokhara.

Tamburlane called for Hafez and said something like: "Do you realize how much wealth and effort I have spent in order to make Bokhara and Samarkand magnificent cities, and you're going to give all that away for a mole?"

Hafez was clearly in danger. He said, "Well, it's by generosity of that sort that I've been reduced to the state that you see me in now." The wit of the answer pleased Tamburlane, and he said something like, "Send this man home with an escort."

Hafez's grasp of metaphor is so delicate and sure that several points of view exist together within a single stanza. He wove the many threads of the Persian poetic tradition into a continuous fabric. Most houses in Iran today will have the collected poems of Hafez on the dining room table. In some families, it is treated as the Chinese used to treat the I Ching; when a family has a problem, they open Hafez's poems at random and see what the ghazal says.

He was an enemy of the mullahs and the ascetics; he makes that clear in virtually every poem. He declares himself on the side of the *rends,* the wild ones or the reprobates, those who wanted to avoid praise for their goodness. He also leaned toward the *malamats,* who would attract public blame in order to lessen self-esteem.

The best supposition is that Hafez died in Shiraz in 1389. At that time there was a serious question as to whether the religious authorities would allow his body to be buried in a Muslim graveyard. It is told that the main mullah of Shiraz had several hundred stanzas of Hafez copied out on small pieces of paper, which were then put into an urn; he ordered a small boy to pick one of them out. The boy picked out this one:

> When Hafez's coffin comes by, it'll be all right
> To follow behind. Although he is
> A captive of sin, he's on his way to the Garden.

That settled it.

All the following ghazals have been done with the generous help of Leonard Lewisohn.

AS RICH AS SOLOMON

Don't expect obedience, promise-keeping, or rectitude
From me; I'm drunk. I have been famous for carrying
A wine pitcher around since the First Covenant with Adam.

That very moment when I cleansed myself in the Spring
Of Love, that very day I said four times
Over the world, as over a corpse, "God is great!"

Give me some wine so I can pass on news of the mystery
Of Fate, and whose face it is with whom I have fallen
In love, and whose fragrance has made me drunk.

The mountain's withers are actually tinier than
The withers of an ant. You who love the fragrance of wine,
Don't lose hope about the door of mercy being open.

Except for the nodding narcissus blossom — may no
Evil eye touch it — no creature has ever been
Really comfortable beneath this turquoise dome.

May my soul be sacrificed to your mouth, because
In the Garden of Contemplation, no bud has ever
Been created by the Gardener of the World sweeter than yours.

Purely because of his love for you, Hafez became
As rich as Solomon; and from his union with you,
Like Solomon, he has nothing but wind in his hands.

#21

THE CRIES WE MAKE

No one has seen your face, and yet a thousand
Doorkeepers have been appointed. You are a closed rose,
And yet a hundred nightingales have arrived.

I may be a long way from you. Let's pray to God
That no human being may be far! But I know
Hope is at hand for a close union with you.

If I should find myself in your neighborhood one day,
That's not strange. For there are in this country,
Thousands of people like me who are strangers.

Is there any lover whose darling never threw
A fond look at his face? There is no pain in you.
With enough pain, the doctor would be here.

In the business of love, there's no great distinction between
The Sufi house and the tavern; in every spot of the universe,
Light shines out from the face of the Friend.

There where the work of the Muslim cloister
Is celebrated, one finds as well the bell
Of the monk's cell and the name of the Cross.

The cries that Hafez has made all of his life
Have not gone to waste; a strange story has emerged
Inside those cries, and a marvelous way of saying.

#64

SITTING IN THE GRIEF HOUSE

Joseph the lost will return, Jacob should not
Sink into sadness; those who sit in the Grief
House will eventually sit in the Garden.

The grieving chest will find honey; do not let
The heart rot. The manic hysterical head
Will find peace — do not sink into sadness.

If the way the Milky Way revolves ignores
Your desires for one or two days, do not
Sink into sadness: all turning goes as it will.

I say to the bird: "As long as Spring
Baptizes the grass, the immense scarlet blossoms
Will continue to sway over your head."

Even if the flood of materialism
Drowns everything, do not sink into
Sadness, because Noah is your captain.

Do not sink into sadness, even though the mysteries
Of the other world slip past you entirely.
There are plays within plays that you cannot see.

When you are far out into the desert, longing
For the Kaaba, and the Arabian thornbush
Pierces your feet, do not sink into sadness.

Although the way station you want to reach
Is dangerous and the goal distant, do not
Sink into sadness: all roads have an end.

God knows our true spiritual state: separated
From Him and punished by rivals. Still do not
Sink into sadness. God is the one who changes conditions.

Oh Hafez in the darkness of poverty and in
The solitude of the night, as long as you can sing
And study the Koran, do not sink into sadness.

#250

THE FIVE DAYS REMAINING

The goods produced in the factories of space and time
Are not all that great. Bring some wine,
Because the desirables of this world are not all that great.

Heart and soul are born for ecstatic conversation
With the soul of souls. That's it. If that fails,
Heart and soul are not in the end that great.

Don't become indebted to the Tuba and Sidra trees
Just to have some shade in heaven. When you look closely,
My flowering cypress friend, you'll see that these trees are not all
    that great.

The true kingdom comes to you without any breaking
Of bones. If that weren't so, achieving the Garden
Through your own labors wouldn't be all that great.

In the five days remaining to you in this rest stop
Before you go to the grave, take it easy, give
Yourself time, because time is not all that great.

You who offer wine, we are waiting on the lip
Of the ocean of ruin. Take this moment as a gift; for the distance
Between the lip and the mouth is not all that great.

The state of my being—miserable and burnt
To a crisp—is proof enough that my need
To put it into words is not all that great.

You ascetic on the cold stone, you are not safe
From the tricks of God's zeal: the distance between the cloister
And the Zoroastrian tavern is not after all that great.

The name of Hafez has been well inscribed in the books,
But in our clan of disreputables, the difference
Between profit and loss is not all that great.

#75

THE STAIN OF THE SEA

Last night I walked sleep-stained to the door
Of the tavern. My prayer rug
And my patched cloak were both stained with wine.

A young Zoroastrian boy stepped tauntingly
From the door; "Wanderer, wake up!"
He said, "The way you walk has the stain of sleep."

Our place is a tavern of ruin, so
Wash in clear water, so that you
Will not leave stains on this holy house.

You are yearning for sweet ruby lips; but
How long will you stain your spiritual
Substance with this sort of ruby?

The way station of old age is one
To pass cleanly; don't let the urgencies
Of youth stain the whiteness of your hair.

The great lovers have found their way
Into the deep ocean, and drowned
Without ever taking one stain from the sea.

Become clean and pure; come up
Out of nature's well! How could
Mud-stained water ever clean your face?

I said to the Soul of the World: "In springtime
Roses are red and drunk. Is there a big problem
Then if my book of roses is stained with wine?"

He replied: "Just cut out selling your friends
These subtle ideas." "Hafez," I said,
"The grace of the teacher is often stained with rebukes."

#414

THE LOST DAUGHTER

Listen to the cry going on at the marketplace
Where lovers lose their souls. All of you who live
In the alley and veer into sin, listen to the cry!

For several days now, the wild daughter has shown
Up missing. She's turned to her own
Affairs; no one knows where. Be alert!

She has a flowing, ruby-colored dress, and bubbles
In her hair. Reason is lost with her, so is learning.
Be careful, beware, your sleep may not be safe.

Whoever brings this bitter one to me, I'll
Repay with halvah as exquisite as your life.
Even though she's gone into the dark, go into hell after her.

She's a night-woman of sharp taste, delicate rosy
Color, and wild and drunk. If you should happen
To find her, please bring her to Hafez's house.

Fragment 19

GABRIEL'S NEWS

Come, come, this Parthenon of desire is set
On wobbly stones. Bring some wine,
For the joists of life are laid on the winds.

The man who can walk beneath the blue wheeling
Heavens and keep his clothes free of the dark
Of attachment—I'll agree to be the slave of his high will.

What can I tell you? Last night at the tavern,
When I was drunk and ruined, what glad news
Did Gabriel bring from the invisible world?

"Your perch is on the lote tree in Paradise,
Oh wide-seeing hawk, what are you doing
Crouching in this mop closet of calamity?

"People on the battlements of heaven are
Blowing a whistle to bring you back.
How does it happen that you tripped the noose?

"I'll give you this advice: Please learn it
And practice it well. These few words
Were given to me by my teacher on the Path.

"Don't expect this rotten world to be faithful
To you. The world we know is a hag
Who has known a thousand husbands.

"Don't let the sorrow of the world bite your soul.
Don't forget what I say. A traveler walking
The road taught me this subtlety about love:

"Be content with what you have now;
Smooth out your forehead. The door of free will
Has never been open for you or for me.

"The smile you see on the face of the rose implies
No promise has been given or kept. Let the nightingale
Lover cry. Cry on. This is a place of wailing."

You writers who write such bad poems, why
Do you envy Hafez so much? His grace of speech
That people love comes entirely from God.

#37

DECIDING NOT TO GO TO INDIA

To spend even one moment grieving about this world
Is a waste of time. Let's go and sell our holy
Robes for wine. A robe does not make one more holy.

It's impossible to buy in the crooked alleys where
The wine sellers hang out even one glass of wine
For a prayer mat. Even a master wouldn't take that deal.

The Zoroastrian tavern keeper says, "You're not worthy
To put your head down on the doorsill." What sort of view of heads
    is this
If the dust on a doorsill is worth more than a head?

Hidden inside the glory of kingship is always
The fear of assassination; a crown is a stylish hat,
But a head is too much to pay for it.

It seemed quite easy to put up with the ocean
And its torments, to receive a profit, but I was wrong;
A hurricane is too much to pay for a hundred pearls.

It's better if you turn your face away from your
Admirers; the joy the general receives from dominating
The world is not worth the suffering of the army.

It's best to aim—as Hafez does—for contentment and abandon
What everyone else wants; one grain of indebtedness
To the base life weighs more than a hundred bushels of gold.

#147

THE FISH IN DEEP WATER

When the one I love takes the cup of wine,
Then the shop of the idols falls to the ground.

I have dropped in a heap on the earth, crying,
In the hope that I will feel a touch of His hand.

I have fallen like a fish into deep water
In the hope that he will throw His net.

Whoever looks into His luminous eyes cries:
"Someone will soon be drunk, get the police!"

How blessèd is the man who, like Hafez,
Has tasted in his heart the wine made before Adam.

#144

THE NIGHT VISIT

Her hair was still tangled, her mouth still drunk
And laughing, her shoulders sweaty, the blouse
Torn open, singing love songs, her wine cup full.

Her eyes were looking for a drunken brawl, her lips
Ready for jibes. She sat down
Last night at midnight on my bed.

She put her lips close to my ear and said
In a whisper these words: "What is this?
Aren't you my old lover—Are you asleep?"

The friend of wisdom who receives
This wine that steals sleep is a traitor to love
If he doesn't worship that same wine.

Oh ascetics, go away. Stop arguing with those
Who drink the bitter stuff, because it was precisely
This gift the divine ones gave us in Pre-Eternity.

Whatever God poured into our goblet
We drank, whether it was the wine
Of heaven or the wine of drunkenness.

The laughter of the wine, and the disheveled curls
Of the Beloved—Oh how many nights of repentance—like
Hafez's—have been broken by moments like this?

#22

NIGHT AND DAWN

Human beings and spirits all take their sustenance
From the existence of love. The practice of devotion
Is a good way to arrive at happiness in both worlds.

Since you aren't worthy of the side glance
She gives, don't try for union. Looking directly
Into Jamshid's cup doesn't work for the blind.

Make an effort, oh Lordly Person, don't miss out
On getting a share of love. No one buys a slave
Who hasn't a single accomplishment of art or grace.

How long will you gobble down the wine of sunrise
And the sugar of dawn sleep? Ask for forgiveness
In the middle of the night and cry when dawn comes.

Come! And with the cash provided by your beauty
Buy the kingdom from us. Don't let this
Slip away; you will regret it if you do.

The prayers of the people who live in corners
Keep disaster away. Why don't you help us
With one single glance out of the corner of your eye?

Both union with you and separation from you
Confuse me. What can I do? You are not present
Nor are you utterly absent from my sight.

A thousand holy souls have been burned up
By this jealousy: you are every dawn and dusk
The candle that's lit in the center of a different group.

Since every bit of news I hear opens a different
Door to bewilderment, from now on I'll take
The road of drunkenness and the path of knowing nothing.

Come, come—the condition of the world as I see it
Is such that if you checked up on it,
You'd sip wine rather than the water of grief.

Because of the good offices of Hafez, we can
Still hope that on some moonlit night we'll
Be able to enjoy our love conversation once more.

ON THE WAY TO THE GARDEN

The garden is breathing out the air of Paradise today;
I sense this friend of heavenly
Nature, and myself, and the genius of the wine.

It's all right if the beggar claims to be a King
Today. His tent is a shadow thrown by a cloud;
The sown field is his room for receiving guests.

The meadow is composing a story of a spring day
In May; the person who knows lets the future
And its profits go and accepts the cash now.

Please don't imagine that your enemy will
Be faithful to you. The candle that stays lit
In the hermit's hut flickers out in the worldly church.

Make your soul strong then by letting it drink
The secret wine. You know that once we're dead,
This rotten world will press our dust into bricks.

My life is a black book. But don't rebuke
Me too much. No one can ever read
The words written on his own forehead.

When Hafez's coffin comes by, it'll be all right
To follow behind. Although he is
A captive of sin, he is on his way to the Garden.

#77

PERMISSIONS

Many of these translations originally appeared in the following books:

Basho: *Basho* (illustrated by Arthur Okamura) (San Francisco: Mudra, 1972).

Gunnar Ekelöf: *Friends, You Drank Some Darkness: Three Swedish Poets: Martinson, Ekelöf, and Tranströmer* (Boston: Beacan Press, 1975); *I Do Best Alone at Night* (with Christina Paulston) (Washington, D.C.: The Charioteer Press, 1968); *Late Arrival on Earth: Selected Poems of Gunnar Ekelöf* (with Christina Paulston) (London: Rapp & Carroll, 1967).

Ghalib: *The Lightning Should Have Fallen on Ghalib: Selected Poems of Ghalib* (with Sunil Dutta) (New York: Ecco Press, 1999).

Hafez: *The Soul Is Here for Its Own Joy: Sacred Poems from Many Cultures* (New York: Ecco Press, 1995).

Olav H. Hauge: *Trusting Your Life to Water and Eternity* (Minneapolis: Milkweed Editions, 1987).

Miguel Hernandez: *Miguel Hernandez and Blas de Otero: Selected Poems,* ed. Timothy Baland and Hardie St. Martin (Boston: Beacon Press, 1972).

Horace: *Horace, the Odes: New Translations by Contemporary Poets,* ed. J. D. McClatchy (Princeton, N.J.: Princeton University Press, 2002); *Horace's Poem on Anger* (Red Wing, Minn.: Red Dragonfly Press, 2000).

Issa: *Ten Poems by Issa* (illustrated by Arthur Okamura) (Point Reyes Station, Calif.: Floating Island Publications, 1992).

Rolf Jacobsen: *The Roads Have Come to an End Now: Selected and Last Poems of Rolf Jacobsen* (with Roger Greenwald and Robert Hedin) (Port Townsend, Wash.: Copper Canyon Press, 2001); *Twenty Poems of Rolf Jacobsen* (Madison, Minn.: Seventies Press, 1977).

Juan Ramón Jiménez: *Lorca and Jiménez: Selected Poems* (Boston: Beacon Press, 1973); *Forty Poems of Juan Ramón Jiménez* (Madison, Minn.: The Sixties Press, 1967).

Kabir: *The Kabir Book* (Boston: Beacon Press, 1977); *Try to Live to See This* (Denver: The Ally Press, 1976); *28 Poems* (New York: Siddha Yoga Dham, 1975); *The Fish in the Sea Is Not Thirsty* (Northwood Narrows, N.H.: Lillabulero Press, 1971).

Federico García Lorca: *Lorca and Jiménez: Selected Poems* (Boston: Beacon Press, 1973).

Antonio Machado: *Times Alone: Selected Poems of Antonio Machado* (Middletown, Conn.: Wesleyan University Press, 1983); *Times Alone* (Port Townsend, Wash.: Graywolf Press, 1982); *Twenty Proverbs* (Marshall, Minn.: Ox Head Press, 1981); *Canciones* (West Branch, Ia.: The Toothpaste Press, 1980); *I Never Wanted Fame* (St. Paul, Minn.: Ally Press, 1979).

Harry Martinson: *Friends, You Drank Some Darkness: Three Swedish Poets: Martinson, Ekelöf, and Tranströmer* (Boston: Beacon Press, 1975).

Mirabai: *Versions* (Penland, N.C.: Squid Ink, 1993); *Mirabai Versions* (The Red Ozier Press, 1980).

Pablo Neruda: *Neruda and Vallejo: Selected Poems* (with John Knoepfle and James Wright) (Boston: Beacon Press, 1971); *Twenty Poems of Pablo Neruda* (with James Wright) (Madison, Minn.: The Sixties Press, 1967).

Francis Ponge: *Ten Poems of Francis Ponge Translated by Robert Bly and Ten Poems of Robert Bly Inspired by the Poems of Francis Ponge* (Riverview, New Brunswick: Owl's Head Press, 1990).

Rainer Maria Rilke: *Selected Poems of Rainer Maria Rilke* (New York: Harper and Row, 1981); *October Day and Other Poems*

(Sebastopol, Calif.: Calliopea Press, 1981); *I Am Too Alone in the World* (New York: The Silver Hands Press, 1980); *The Voices* (Denver: The Ally Press, 1977); *Ten Sonnets to Orpheus,* printed in *Zephyrus Image Magazine* (1), 1972.

Rumi: *Night and Sleep* (with Coleman Barks) (Cambridge, Mass.: Yellow Moon Press, 1981); *When Grapes Turn to Wine* (Cambridge, Mass.: Yellow Moon Press, 1986).

Georg Trakl: *Twenty Poems of George Trakl* (with James Wright) (Madison, Minn.: The Sixties Press, 1961).

Tomas Tranströmer: *The Half-Finished Heaven: The Best Poems of Tomas Tranströmer* (St. Paul, Minn.: Graywolf Press, 2001); *Truth Barriers* (San Francisco: Sierra Club Books, 1980); *Friends, You Drank Some Darkness: Three Swedish Poets: Martinson, Ekelöf, and Tranströmer* (Boston: Beacon Press, 1975); *Night Vision* (Northwoods Narrows, N.H.: Lillabulero Press, 1971); *Twenty Poems of Tomas Tranströmer* (Madison, Minn.: The Seventies Press, 1970).

Cesar Vallejo: *Neruda and Vallejo: Selected Poems* (with John Knoepfle and James Wright) (Boston: Beacon Press, 1971); *Twenty Poems of Cesar Vallejo* (with John Knoepfle and James Wright) (Madison, Minn.: The Sixties Press, 1962).

We are grateful to these publishers and editors for permission to publish translations here.

INDEX